The
Sleuth's Surprise

The
Sleuth's Surprise
The Librarian Sleuth—Book Four

By
Kimberly Rose Johnson

The Sleuth's Surprise
Published by Mountain Brook Ink
White Salmon, WA U.S.A.

The website addresses shown in this book are not intended in any way to be or imply an endorsement on the part of Mountain Brook Ink, nor do we vouch for their content.

This story is a work of fiction. All characters and events are the product of the author's imagination other than those stated in the author notes as based on historical characters. Any other resemblance to any person, living or dead, is coincidental.

Scripture quotations are taken from the King James Version of the Bible. Public domain.

The Team: Miralee Ferrell, Alyssa Roat, Cindy Jackson
Cover Design: Indie Cover Design, Lynnette Bonner Designer

Mountain Brook Ink is an inspirational publisher offering fiction you can believe in.

Printed in the United States of America

Acknowledgements

As with most big things this book took many hands to make it what it is today. I'd like to take a moment to thank my editor and publisher, Miralee Ferrell, for her dedication to publishing entertaining and quality books. Special thanks to all of the proofreaders who took the time to make sure this book is as mistake free as possible.

Finally, thank you to my family, specifically my husband, for your support and confidence in my writing. Without your confidence and continued encouragement this wouldn't be nearly as much fun.

Chapter One

Nancy Daley Malone stared at the newspaper in disbelief. She held it up and waved it at Pepper White, her good friend and owner of Roaster's Coffee Shop. "Did you see this?"

"No. What is it?" Pepper slid a plate with a chocolate donut onto the table in front of Nancy then sat across from her.

"Someone is running for sheriff against my mom."

"Ah, that. Yes, I did hear some rumblings."

"Why didn't you say anything?"

Pepper shrugged. "I figured you already knew. You seem to always know everything that goes on in this town."

Nancy frowned. "Not this time."

"Your mom is scrappy. She'll win back the community's support."

A jolt shot through Nancy. "Win back?" What was her friend talking about? The town respected and loved her mom. Didn't they?

"Well, there's been some talk that maybe she doesn't have a good handle on things anymore. I overheard someone in here the other day suggest she's become too comfortable."

"That's ridiculous!" Nancy's face heated. She stood. "I need to go."

Pepper reached out and touched Nancy's arm. "I'm sorry. I probably should have told you sooner or not at all. Please don't leave angry."

Nancy stilled. "I'm not angry with you. I wish you would have said something when you first heard what people were saying, but I don't hold it against you. I'm galvanized to do something to help my mom. People are wrong about her, and I want them to know it."

"Ah, I see. Okay. Let me know how I can help."

"Thanks."

Pepper reached for the plate with Nancy's treat. "What about your donut?"

"I can't eat right now." Her stomach was as knotted as the cord of her ear buds.

"At least take it with you." Pepper wrapped the donut in a napkin and handed it to her. "I know you'll want it later."

Nancy eyed the donut—her once a week ritual she shared with her good friend. "Good idea. You're probably right. Thanks." She dropped the treat into her oversized purse and headed for the door. She'd show Tipton County they were wrong about her mom if it was the last thing she did.

Lyle Griffin dropped today's paper on the sheriff's desk. "You're going to want to see this." He glanced toward the small egress window in the basement office as someone walked past.

Sheriff Daley looked up from her computer screen and picked up the paper. Her brows rose. "How did I not know this?"

"I don't think anyone knew. That's Stan Gibson's official announcement." For the first time since Mary Daley had been elected, she had an opponent. Lyle had heard rumblings that the community was unhappy with the uptick in crime, and several citizens were blaming the sheriff. As if she had anything to do with it. "What are you going to do?"

She handed him back the paper. "I guess run a campaign. I've never had to do that while in office."

"Won't be easy, as hands-on as you are."

"Agreed. But if I want to keep my job, it looks like I'll have to figure out how to do everything while running a winning campaign as well."

He eased into the chair across from her desk. "What can I do to help?" He did not want to work for Stan. The man seemed nice enough, but to his knowledge, Stan knew nothing about law enforcement, which begged the question how he was even qualified to be sheriff.

"I'm not sure what kind of help I need. It's been a long time since I had to campaign."

"How long has it been?"

"Twenty-five years."

"You could retire." As soon as he said the words, he wanted to snatch them back. "I didn't mean that the way it sounded. I only mean that you've been in law enforcement long enough to retire with benefits." Mary was in the prime of her life at fifty-five. Her coffee-colored hair only had a smattering of gray. Though her face had begun to show her years of service, she still looked vibrant to him.

Her brown eyes flashed annoyance then softened. "Thanks for clarifying."

He shrugged. "You've earned the right to retire."

"You didn't walk away when you reached twenty years."

"I wasn't ready." But should Stan win the election, he'd definitely give that option consideration. Lots of people reinvented themselves. There was nothing stopping him from doing the same.

Mary sighed. "I was invited to be the local celebrity judge at the Tipton County Fair's pie-baking. I'd planned to decline, but it would be a good opportunity for me to rub shoulders with the community. What do you think?"

Lyle knew she hated that kind of thing and certainly didn't need one more stress added to her life, but if she wanted to win, this was the perfect opportunity to connect with the community on a social level. "It's a great idea. I can come along if you want company. Maybe hand out buttons or something with your face on them."

She chuckled. "The obligatory buttons. I'd forgotten about those. If you'd like to go, that'd be nice, but it's not necessary. I'm sure Nancy will want to be there, so don't feel obligated."

"I wouldn't miss it." The sheriff had done a good job raising her daughter, and if anyone could influence the community to vote for Mary, it was Nancy. The people in Tipton loved her. He'd do about anything for both mother and daughter. They were like family—the family he'd never had but dreamed of.

He stood and moved toward the door to her office. "Tell you what. I'll talk to Nancy, and we'll figure out a plan. We can't let Stan beat you, unless you're ready to move on."

"I'm not."

Lyle grinned. "Neither am I, boss." They had a good working relationship, and he'd miss her more than he could bear if she wasn't here.

"Good." She chuckled. "Now that we have that settled, get to work."

She might sound stern, but she was as soft as a caramel deep down. "Let me know how I can help." He moseyed out of her office.

Still stunned that her position as sheriff was being challenged, Mary closed her eyes and took a cleansing breath. *Lord, if you want me to stay on as sheriff, I'm going to need your help.*

Her phone rang. She checked the caller ID and sighed before answering and putting on her most chipper voice. "Good morning, Mayor Wallace."

"No need to be so formal, Mary. I've told you to call me Charlie at least a hundred times."

"And I've told you, I prefer to be addressed as Sheriff."

He cleared his throat. "About that. Have you read the morning paper?"

"I have. Thanks for the heads up." *Not.*

"It was a matter of public record. All you had to do was look to see who had filed."

She rolled her eyes. She wasn't in the mood to be talked down to. "Does he even have the right credentials? He's a high school English teacher."

"Believe it or not, he does. Before Stan moved to Tipton, he was in law enforcement."

"How? He can't be over thirty. He has a master's in education, so how is it he had time to do both?"

"Guess he's an overachiever. I actually called to talk with you about the pie judging. You never said if you're onboard or not."

"I'm looking forward to it." Okay, so maybe that was a stretch, but she enjoyed pie. How much of a trial could it be?

"That's what I was hoping to hear." He actually sounded gleeful.

Mary narrowed her eyes. "You are way too happy about this. What's going on?"

"I thought it'd be fun for the community to see you and Stan side-by-side at the fair."

"Please tell me this is a joke." It wasn't that she minded sharing the job, it was the person she had to share it with that was the problem—her running mate.

"Now, Mary."

"Sheriff." She had no idea why it bothered her so much for him to use her given name, but it was like fingernails on a chalkboard on the annoyance level.

"Sorry, *Sheriff*. This isn't a joke. I realize Stan isn't a celebrity, but he's a popular teacher, and the high school students will eat this up. No pun intended."

"Then why not get another teacher to judge and leave me out of it?" She wanted to snatch the words back as soon as they popped out. She didn't need her competition to have the upper hand in the eyes of the public.

"That's an option, but this would be much more interesting."

"Fine. Count me in." She had a feeling she might regret agreeing to judge the pie-baking contest, but her instinct said it was the right thing to do.

"Excellent." Muffled voices sounded in the

background on his end of the phone call. "I need to go. I'll email you the specifics."

She hung up the receiver. A commotion in the bullpen grabbed her attention. She stood and stepped out of her office. "Nancy." Her daughter had a way of causing a ruckus on a good day, but today was anything but.

"Mom. Did you see this?" She waved a newspaper in the air as she stood on the other side of the reception counter. Nancy had a habit of thinking the sheriff's department was her own personal space to come and go as she pleased. Mary had informed Lyle to put a stop to it a while back, but in this case, she wanted her daughter here. "Please come into my office."

Winnie, the receptionist, buzzed her in.

Nancy strode across the bullpen like she belonged—no wonder, since she was the daughter of the sheriff and the wife of Deputy Malone. "I came right over from Roaster's as soon as I saw this."

"You cut out early on your weekly girl time with Pepper?" She frowned. Her daughter lived, ate, and breathed work, but she religiously kept their long-standing tradition.

"Of course. I had to see you. Are you okay?"

"I'm a big girl, Nancy. I can handle a little competition." At least she hoped so. She'd heard rumors about disgruntled townspeople. Why did they blame her for the uptick in crime? It wasn't like she put an ad in the paper encouraging thieves and druggies to come to Tipton County. On top of that, her department had a good record for convictions sticking in court. Didn't the community understand that? Apparently not, according to the rumbles she'd heard about town.

Nancy reached into her purse and pulled out a chocolate donut and placed it on her desk. "You're not upset?"

"I'm not happy that I will have to divide my time with the election, but we can do this. In fact, I'll be judging the pie-baking contest at the fair next weekend. It should make for a good photo op and allow me to mingle with everyday folks."

Wonder settled on Nancy's face. "You are taking this amazingly well, Mom. I was so upset for you, but now that I see you're fine..." she reached for her donut and took a large bite. The tension that had been on her face moments ago vanished.

Mary chuckled. "You and chocolate."

"It's not dark chocolate, but a donut works in a pinch." Nancy devoured the donut.

A rap on her door drew their attention. Her son-in-law Carter Malone stood in the doorway. "I heard you were here. Is everything okay?"

"Not exactly," Nancy said. "But nothing is wrong."

His forehead wrinkled. "You're not making sense."

"Stan Gibson, a teacher at Tipton High, is running against Mom."

His frown deepened. "So it's true." He looked at Mary. "What's your plan?"

"My plan is to win." The people of Tipton County had to see that her experience in law enforcement for the past twenty-five years was invaluable compared to a relative newbie. Stan couldn't have more than two years in law enforcement.

Nancy stood and paced to the tiny window to the alley where only feet could be seen walking past from time to time. She whirled around to face them. "We need to take advantage of every opportunity for the citizens of Tipton County to see you out and about. You've been too cooped up in this building or out on calls. People need to see you among them."

"The county fair next week will be a step in that direction." Gratitude for such an amazing and supportive daughter almost overwhelmed her, and she blinked back tears. What was up with that? She wasn't an emotional person. Could the election, along with everything else, be pushing her to her limit and making her teary? She prayed not. That surely wouldn't instill confidence in the citizens of Tipton if they caught her crying. Good thing she was in the privacy of her office and not out on the street right now.

Nancy nodded distractedly. "Yes, but that's not enough. We should have dinner at different places around town. We can start at Maggie's Pizza tonight. It's always busy on Friday nights."

Her daughter was like a hurricane when she put her mind to something—there was no stopping her. "I'm off at six. I'll meet you there shortly after, assuming I'm not dealing with a crime somewhere."

Nancy looked at her husband. "Are you going to join us?"

"If I can, I'll be there."

Nancy grinned. "Perfect." She glanced at the time. "I need to open the library. Keep me in the loop if anything changes."

"I'll see you out." Carter rested his hand at the base of Nancy's back as they walked through the bullpen.

Mary sighed and returned to the paperwork awaiting her attention. This was going to be a long few months. Now if Tipton could only escape any major crimes, she should have a chance at keeping her job.

Chapter Two

One week later

MARY STOOD IN THE DESIGNATED TENT for the pie contest. Heat engulfed her. Why, oh why did they hold this inside a tent in the middle of summer? Lyle had sent a text stating he'd be late. Lucky him. He wouldn't be in the stifling heat so long.

Mayor Wallace looked her direction from his position beside the pie table and waved. She raised a hand in greeting then noted the crowd of women gathered around the pie table. It seemed this was the place to be.

Laura, Nancy's assistant, was there with her little girl. Pepper from the coffee shop held what looked to be a berry pie. Gloria Davis, Tipton's most vocal philanthropist, spoke with the mayor's daughter, May, and even Traci from dispatch was there along with several other women.

She narrowed her eyes. Was that Philomena? A shudder shook her. Philomena Cartwright had been a thorn in her side since the day Mary had become sheriff more than two decades ago. The sixty-something-year-old woman constantly interfered with the raising of Nancy. Her jaw tightened, thinking about that woman—talk about a busy body.

Philomena spotted her and headed in her direction. Mary simply couldn't deal with the woman's self-righteous attitude today. She looked around for a place to hide.

"Sheriff Daley." Philomena waved.

Mary stifled a groan. She was too late to escape.

Philomena flounced to a stop in front of her and peered at her with her hawk-like eyes. "I heard you're a judge this year. Are you sure your taste buds are up to the task?"

"My taste buds haven't failed me yet." Mary plastered on a smile. She would not let this woman ruin her day.

"Well, I'm sure you're going to love my strawberry rhubarb pie."

"Oh, you have a pie in the contest?" Mary asked.

"Now, Philomena." Mayor Charlie tugged at her arm. "You shouldn't be talking with one of the judges before the contest." He pulled her away.

Philomena tossed a look over her shoulder that Mary couldn't decipher—odd even for Philomena.

Mary shivered in spite of the heat in the tent. That woman was something else. She owed Mayor Charlie for rescuing her. Mary blew out a breath and looked around for Stan. Where could he be? Hopefully he wouldn't be late. She'd skipped breakfast and hadn't had time for lunch. Her stomach growled. "Please let the pies be good," she said under her breath.

She'd heard rumors that a couple of the ladies who entered pies should never step foot in a kitchen much less bake for a contest. Based on the women gathered near the table, she had hope for several good slices. Pepper made exceptional baked goods.

Nancy sidled up to her. "You ready for this?"

"Ready as I'll ever be." She fanned her hand in front of her face. "You'd think they could set up a couple of fans or something. It's stifling."

"I got you covered." Nancy pulled a small fan with a water bottle connected to it from her oversized purse. "You can set this on the table when you're judging to help cool you off."

"You're the best daughter a woman could ask for."

"Ha, you say that now, but wait until I do something to aggravate you."

Mary chuckled. Nancy did have a way of inserting herself into cases she had no business being a part of, but it was her own fault for allowing her daughter to consult on the lesser crimes. She looked around the tent, hoping Lyle had made it. Having his and Nancy's moral support meant a lot.

Nancy held up a bag. "I had buttons made that say Mary Daley for Sheriff." She pulled one out. "What do you think?"

Mary tried not to cringe. It felt so cheesy to hand out buttons, but that's what they did in Tipton. "Looks great." She took the button her daughter held. "Guess I should wear one."

Nancy grinned. "Me too." She pinned it to her tank top.

"I suppose I should mingle. Are you sticking around for the judging?"

"I wouldn't miss it. I have 9-1-1 on speed dial in case you or Stan are poisoned."

"Not funny."

"I'm not joking." She lowered her voice. "I heard the last person who judged had to have their stomach pumped."

Nausea hit Mary—she should have at least eaten breakfast. "I'm sure that's an exaggeration." At least she hoped it was. "Here goes nothing." She raised her chin slightly and walked across the space to the pie table against the far tent wall where a small crowd of women and one man gathered.

Mayor Wallace cleared his throat. "We are about to begin. Has anyone seen Stan?"

Mary turned and looked around the tent as Stan sauntered in. "He just arrived."

"If I may have a word." The mayor motioned her to follow him. He waited for Stan to join them. "Here's how this will work. I will present each of you with a tray of pie slices. You will take one bite of every slice, but you are not required to swallow. Napkins and water are provided." He looked over his shoulder then lowered his voice. "I suggest not swallowing if it tastes bad. That's what the pile of napkins are for."

Stan shook his head. "It would be rude to do that." He glanced at Mary. "I don't know about you, but this is good PR for me, and I'm not going to offend these bakers by spitting out their creations."

"I agree." The idea was ludicrous. Nancy's warning tickled the back of her mind. She pushed the thought away.

"It's your choice." Charlie went on to explain the judging forms. "Any questions?"

"Seems clear to me." Apprehension filled Mary. She really didn't want food poisoning. Maybe she should take advantage of those napkins—no, she couldn't risk offending anyone. She liked her job and aimed to keep it for at least one more term. She'd taste every single entry with a smile, regardless of the consequences.

"Good. I'll be right back with your pie slices."

Stan sat beside her at the judges' table. "I hope there are no hard feelings about me running against you."

"Why would I have hard feelings? After all, I've only been in law enforcement for twenty-five years and invested my life into this town."

Stan had the grace to look embarrassed. "I realize Tipton County is important to you, and it is to me as well. I want you to know, should I win, I will do my best to serve as well as you have these past two plus decades."

Mary tilted her head. "You sound like you mean that."

"I do. Law enforcement is in my blood."

"I heard you were a cop once. Why are you teaching English?"

"Long story short. I wanted to be a cop, but my mom encouraged me, rather strongly, to go into education. She's a teacher too. My dad, however, was a cop. When he was killed in the line of duty, I went back to school for my masters so I could teach. My mom was a wreck and couldn't handle me being in law enforcement after Dad died."

Mary nodded. Now it made sense. "What changed?"

"My mom passed away six months ago. Now I can follow my heart again."

"I'm sorry about your mother."

"Thanks."

"You don't like teaching?"

He shrugged. "I loved it my first year. But dealing with parents and the school politics was a pain."

Mary chuckled. "Multiply that by one hundred for this job." She ought to know, she had the frequent high blood pressure to prove it. "Are you sure you want to be sheriff? Deputy positions open up from time to time."

Uncertainty crossed his face. "Only once since I've been in town."

"Here we go." Donning gloves, Mayor Wallace, placed a tray onto the table. "Those are for you, Mary. I'll be right back with yours, Stan."

"Gloves?" Mary asked. "Isn't that a bit much?"

"I was told I had to wear them. Isn't it some health code?"

Mary shrugged. "I was teasing." Though she should know, she had no idea if the law required him to wear gloves. She glanced at Stan.

Disappointment filled his eyes.

Mary slid the tray his direction. "Go for it. I don't mind waiting for the next batch. You look like you want these more than I do."

"You sure? Believe it or not, I've been looking forward to this all week. Even knowing some of them won't be good."

"Positive. Enjoy." She chuckled.

Like a man-child in his enthusiasm, Stan started at the top left corner of the tray and forked a bite of apple pie into his mouth. "Mmm. This is great." He filled out the judging form then moved on to the next piece. There were ten entries total.

A crashing sound drew her attention toward the pie table. The tray of pie slices she was to judge lay upside down on the ground.

Utter silence filled the tent as all heads swiveled toward Charlie and his daughter May, who must have dropped the tray, based on her flaming cheeks.

"No worries. I'll cut more." The mayor quickly got busy slicing more pie while May cleared the mess.

"At this rate I'll be finished judging by the time you get yours. I'm sure glad you let me go first. These pies are really good." Stan dug into the next piece—strawberry rhubarb. The man judged each bite in under ten seconds then moved on to the next slice.

Mary's mouth began to water. She eyed the mixed berry entry—her favorite. And if she wasn't mistaken, Pepper had made it. Her gaze drifted over the tray. Then again, the chocolate cream looked delectable. What was taking Charlie so long? Okay, so maybe it hadn't been that long, but her stomach was growling. Sitting close enough to smell the pies was torture.

Stan only had one piece left to judge. Great, all eyes would be on her as she judged. At least he seemed to have liked all of them. Maybe the bad bakers hadn't entered this year.

"How were they?" She asked out of the side of her mouth.

"Actually, most of them were pretty good." Stan grinned.

A minute later Mayor Wallace placed her tray of pie slices onto the table. "Sorry for the delay." His eyes widened. "That first tray was for you, Sheriff." A note of panic crossed his face.

Odd. It's not like it mattered. All the slices came from the same pies. She shrugged. "Stan was drooling, so I gave him the first batch."

"But I was given specific instructions."

"My whom?" She couldn't imagine why it would matter.

"An email." He shook his head. "Sorry. Ignore me. I'm a rule follower, but even I don't see why it should matter. Enjoy."

"Thanks. I'm sure I will." She smiled as she raised her fork. "So they were pretty good, huh?" She tilted her head toward Stan and stilled.

He ran his finger along the top of his collar. His face flushed. He looked to be having trouble breathing.

Something was clearly wrong. "Are you okay?" She placed a hand on his arm.

He pushed back from the table, stood halfway, then fell to the ground unconscious.

"Nancy, call 9-1-1." Mary dropped to the ground beside Stan. His labored breathing became weaker with every passing second. "Hang in there, Stan. Help is on the way. Do you have a food allergy? An EpiPen?"

He shook his head and gasped for air. "Can't breathe."

She pulled out her phone and called Lyle. "I need you at the County Fair immediately. Come to the pie tent."

"I'm almost there. What's up?"

"Just get here and use your siren."

"I'm literally at the park. I'll be right there." He disconnected the call.

Stan stopped breathing. Unease shot through Mary. She felt for a pulse—nothing. She began chest compressions.

Nancy squatted beside her. "An ambulance is on the way."

"Let's hope they hurry." Mary continued chest compressions. Though she wasn't sure it would do any good, she had to try.

Lyle burst into the tent. He rushed to Mary's side. "What happened?"

Mary kept her voice low. "I'm not sure, but I think he was either poisoned or had an allergic reaction to one of the pies—though he said he wasn't allergic to anything." Her breath shuddered as she released it. "It happened so fast. One minute he was smiling and saying how good the pies were, then next he was having trouble breathing."

Lyle took over chest compressions.

Five minutes later after no change, Mary rested a hand on Lyle's shoulder. "You can stop. He's gone." If she'd eaten the pie from that tray... Her gaze shot to the table where a woman she didn't recognize reached for the remaining tray. "Don't touch that!"

The mousey, blonde-haired woman dropped it and stepped back.

Mary would have to find out who she was later.

"He's dead?" Shock filled Nancy's voice. "So fast? Did he have a heart attack?"

"I don't think so." Mary could only think of one thing that would kill a man in less than five minutes—cyanide.

Nancy whispered. "You think he was poisoned?"

Mary pursed her lips and nodded once. "I need to secure the scene and get the medical examiner over here." She stood and realized for the first time that most of the people in the tent were standing around the crime scene. "Everyone please take a seat. Stan had a medical emergency, and we need you to stay back." She herded the crowd toward the seating area.

"What happened?" Maggie, the owner of Maggie's pizza, asked. "Why did you stop CPR?"

"Stan is…dead," Nancy declared.

A collective gasp sounded and then a roar of voices.

Mary strode to her daughter and tugged her away from Stan. "You're going to cause a panic."

"I'm sorry. I wasn't thinking. This is all such a shock." Nancy lowered her voice and spoke into her mom's ear. "I've read that cyanide has a faint, bitter almond scent. Did you smell it?"

Mary shook her head. "No, but I figured it had to be cyanide from the symptoms and how fast he passed. I wish you'd kept quiet about his death. Now we have pandemonium, and I only have Lyle to help."

"Carter should be here any second."

"Good." Nancy's husband was the best detective they had.

"Ladies and gentlemen, if you would all take a seat please." Mary pulled out her phone and took pictures of those in attendance. Hopefully, no one had slipped away already. Was the killer still here? Was the killer ever here?

Mary then turned and took pictures of the crime scene. Had Stan really been murdered or was there another explanation? She couldn't recall anyone dying of natural causes in that way.

Carter strode into the tent and quickly assessed the situation before approaching her. "What can I do?"

"I want all the pies, including the slices at the judges' table, taken into evidence. They need to be tested for poison."

The paramedics arrived and confirmed Stan was deceased. The next two hours were a blur of activity. Lightheaded and in desperate need of food, Mary left the tent. A fruit stand caught her eye. She purchased a container of grapes and found a bench in the shade. Someone had tried to kill her. Stan's body would be autopsied to confirm, but she knew in her gut what the examiner would find—cyanide—meant for her.

Lyle sat beside Mary on the shade-covered bench, looking wearier than he'd ever seen her. "How're you holding up?"

"I've been better."

"I imagine so." He had no idea what to say to this woman who was not only his boss but also the only woman he'd ever cared about. He'd been walking a tightrope for years. She didn't return his affection and couldn't so long as she was his boss. Although he was perturbed when he learned Stan was challenging her for the sheriff position, over the past week he'd come to secretly hope the man would win so he could finally ask Mary out.

Now Stan was dead, and Lyle's stomach was a bundle of knots.

"Whatever killed Stan was intended for me." Her shoulders hunched forward slightly.

"Come again?" His pulse amped. "Are you certain?"

She nodded.

Mary was in danger, and she was sitting out in the open? Was she in shock? He studied her face a moment—definitely not herself. She lacked her normal zest and confidence. Stan's death had shaken her to her core.

He scanned the area for anyone who looked suspicious. The fair goers didn't pay them any special attention.

Mary sighed. "Charlie was instructed to give me the first tray. He'd said as much too, but then let it go. I should have questioned him right away, but I've been so busy, I forgot to ask him who told him I was to get that tray."

"I'll talk to him. He's still in the tent pacing."

"Pacing?" Mary looked toward the tent.

"Yeah. I think maybe he feels responsible since he's the Mayor. But it's kind of odd if you ask me."

"Indeed. Maybe we both ought to go and question him." Mary stood.

"Hold on a minute. All things considered, I think you should head home. Clear your head."

"No time. I don't want to end up in the morgue beside Stan. The sooner we figure out who killed him the better."

He nodded. "Understood." He might understand her desire to investigate the crime, but he didn't like it. Not one bit. "But, Sheriff, ask yourself this; if things were different and one of your deputies was in the same position you find yourself in now, wouldn't you insist he went home?"

She narrowed her eyes. "I'm not one of my deputies." Her steely tone left no room for argument.

He raised his hands in surrender. "It's your life."

He strode toward the tent and realized Mary wasn't with him. He turned back. She stood beside the bench unmoving. He strode back to her. "You coming?"

"I'm not feeling very well. Maybe I should go home after all."

His heart pounded. "What did you eat?"

"Only some grapes. There's no way they were poisoned."

He reached for her arm. "I think you should go to the hospital to be safe."

She stepped back, avoiding his attempt to escort her to his vehicle. "No. I haven't eaten all day. Grapes have a lot of sugar."

"Which upsets your stomach." He knew Mary well, and she couldn't stomach a lot of sugar, begging the question why she hadn't thought to eat before the contest. "You're a glutton for punishment today."

"Definitely not one of my better days. If you have everything under control here, I'll go and grab a solid meal."

"You can count on Carter and me to make sure everything here is done right."

"I know. Thanks, Lyle. Call me later with an update."

He nodded.

She turned and walked away without looking back.

He set his jaw and strode toward the tent. He had a killer to find before the killer struck again.

Later that night Lyle sank into his favorite easy chair. It creaked with age, like his knees, but he didn't care. It fit him perfectly. He closed his eyes in an attempt to focus his thoughts. He needed to give Mary an update, but he didn't have much to report. She wasn't going to be happy.

Thankfully, he and Carter had managed to keep the fact that the pie had been meant for her mother from Nancy, although he imagined she'd figure it out on her own before long. That girl was like her mom in so many ways. He'd expected her to follow in her mother's footsteps and go into law enforcement too, but her love of books won. Then again, in a way she had a hand in law enforcement, though not officially. Nancy never met a mystery she couldn't solve.

He sighed and opened his eyes—time to call Mary. He placed the call.

She answered on the first ring. "What do you know?"

"Actually, quite a lot. But I imagine you're talking about the case. We're still waiting on the toxicology report from the pies and the medical examiner's report."

"What about suspects?"

"We don't have a cause of death—probably poisoning—but there's a chance this wasn't murder."

"Slight."

He couldn't argue that. His gut said Stan was murdered, and based on what Mary said, the evidence would support it. "I spoke with Charlie. He didn't remember who told him you were to receive the first tray."

"Maybe he will when *I* ask him."

He knew that tone. Mary was rearing for a battle. "Speaking as your friend and not your employee, I hope you will temper that fight I hear in your voice.

Attacking the mayor won't get you anywhere."

She sighed. "I know. I'm letting my frustration get the best of me."

"I understand." He'd been fighting the same thing ever since he'd started this investigation. "We'll figure this out and when we do, whoever is behind this will pay."

"But will we find the perpetrator before he strikes again?"

Chapter Three

MONDAY AFTERNOON NANCY SAT BEHIND THE circulation desk at Tipton County Library. After the crazy weekend at the fair, the calm of the library was exactly what she needed—that and chocolate. She slid open the top drawer of her desk and popped a candy kiss into her mouth. The tension in her shoulders eased.

Laura Stanley, her new library assistant, strode across the blue concrete floor toward her, pushing an almost empty book cart. She stopped beside the circulation desk. "I found a couple of books that need to be mended. Would you like me to take care of them before I head out to pick up Clair?"

Nancy glanced at the wall clock and nodded. "That would be great." Laura would take a break at three-fifteen to pick up her darling daughter from daycare, then they'd both come back until the end of the day for the story time Laura had organized.

Nancy found a gem when she hired the thirty-something woman. She really connected with the younger patrons. Best yet, she was competent and could run the library without her. Though Nancy missed Tara, her former assistant, she didn't compare to Laura when it came to initiative and instinct on how to make the library the best it could be. The woman knew what she was doing.

The library doors slid open, and Carter sauntered

in, wearing his deputy uniform and looking as handsome as ever. Somehow his blue eyes looked even bluer this afternoon. Her heart skipped a beat at the sight of her husband. She stood and smiled. "This is a nice surprise. What brings you by?"

"I wanted to deliver this news in person." He looked around and lowered his voice. "The toxicology report came back on the pies. Only one slice of pie had been poisoned. It was cyanide. Which, as you probably already know, would kill a person if certain forms of it got on their skin, much less ingested it."

"Was this that kind of cyanide?" Instinct told her it was, but she needed to hear him say it.

He nodded. "Yes. We are fortunate no one else was killed. Whoever did this wasn't taking any chances they'd accomplish their goal."

Nancy frowned. "Any idea whose pie it was?"

He nodded. "I will question her today, but do you think someone would poison the pie they entered?"

"That would be kind of dumb since they'd be the first suspect. Out of curiosity whose entry was it?"

A pained look covered his face. "Pepper."

Nancy gasped. "You know she'd never do that, right?"

"Of course. More than likely, it wasn't even someone who had a pie in the contest."

"I don't know. Seems to me any one of the pie entrants had opportunity."

"Based on your own words Pepper is at least a person of interest."

She waved a hand. "Pff. Cross her off your list. You said yourself, you didn't think she did it. She'd never kill anyone."

"She's already crossed off. I spoke with her yesterday, and it was obvious she had nothing to do with it."

"Who else have you questioned?"

"I really shouldn't say. Your mom doesn't want you involved in this."

Her eyes widened. "That first tray was intended for my mom." It wasn't a question. "I saw Charlie place it in front of her and overheard him say it was for her." She hadn't considered the possibility that her mom had been the target until a moment ago.

"You're good." His eyes shone with admiration. "It appears someone wants your mom out of the picture." He made the face that said he was going to say something he didn't think she'd like. "There's more."

More? Nancy sat down in her chair. "I'm ready. What is it?"

"She asked me to run against her for sheriff."

"What?" Her voice rose an octave. "Why would she do that? She's uncontested as it stands now."

He put a finger to his lips. "Shh."

She ducked her head and brought her volume back down to a whisper. "Sorry. What are you going to do?"

"I never aspired to be the sheriff."

She knew the toll being sheriff took on her mother and didn't want that for her husband. Especially when they were still newlyweds. "I'll talk to her."

"No. You need to stay out of this."

Her head jerked back. "Why?"

"Because you need to distance yourself from her

for your own protection. I only told you what I did because I want you to be careful. They might try to get to your mom through you."

She crossed her arms. She didn't like the sound of that one bit.

Laura slid behind her and pulled her purse from a drawer. "Don't mind me. I'll be back soon."

"Thanks, Laura." Nancy spared her a glance.

Carter nodded at her assistant then returned his attention to Nancy. "You might think my request is unwarranted, but until we know more, it's for the best. Your mom and I need to be able to do our jobs without worrying about you."

"I'm a grown woman, not a child. You don't need to worry about me." This had been an issue for them practically since they'd met, and though his love and concern endeared him to her, it was unnecessary. She could take care of herself—the same could have been said of Stan too, though. "Forget I said that. I promise to be careful. What are you going to do about running for sheriff?"

"I'm still thinking."

"What does Lyle say?"

"She asked him to run against her first. He refused."

"Oh." Lyle would probably win if he had agreed to it. He'd been part of the Tipton community for as long as her mom and would make an exceptional sheriff. "Do you want to be sheriff?"

"I'm warming to the idea, but I'm happy with my current position. I'm not sure how Gavin would handle it if I became sheriff."

His nephew was definitely a consideration. "I

think you need to talk to him before you jump into this."

"The deadline to enter is today at five."

"Then you better get moving."

"Are you okay with me running?"

Her knee-jerk response was no, but that wasn't fair to Mom or Carter. "I think you need to do what you want to do."

"If I actually win, it will mean some changes for us."

"I know, but I don't want to hold you back if this is what you want." But if he won, would her mom resent him, even though it was her idea?

He tilted his head. "You're not being helpful."

"You have my support no matter what. But know I'll also be rooting for my mom."

"Guess you can't lose then." He chuckled. "I'll see you tonight." He placed a peck on her lips and turned to leave right as Laura and her daughter Clair entered with her blonde pigtails bouncing on each side of her face.

"Hi, Deputy Malone." Clair skipped over to him. "Are you here for story time?"

"I'm afraid not. Have fun." He looked over his shoulder and sent a longing look at Nancy.

Her breath caught. What did that look mean?

Later in the afternoon Nancy power walked beside Anna, one of her best friends. Freddy, Anna's American Eskimo dog, pranced beside her. "May I ask your advice about something?"

"Of course." Anna slid a glance her way. The woman had morphed into a beautiful butterfly since they'd started walking together. Funny how fresh air and a little exercise could make such a difference in a person. Of course love had something to do with that too.

"Early this afternoon Carter came by the library, and right before he left, he shot me a strange look—longing is the best way I can describe it."

"Shocker."

Nancy chuckled. "Oh, stop. Not that kind of longing. What's up? It's not like you to be snarky."

"Sorry. It's been one of those days. Luke is beside himself."

"Because of Stan's death?" Anna's boyfriend was the head of the English department where they both taught English. "I wonder why Stan didn't resign since he was running for sheriff."

"They had a plan in place, but now the school doesn't have much time to find a replacement before classes next month."

"I'm surprised his position hadn't already been filled since he was running for office."

Anna shrugged. "Luke said since he wouldn't have started until January. They agreed during contract time to let him work the first semester while they sought to find his replacement if he won the election. Now they've been forced to move the timeline up by several months."

"Ah. Now I see."

Anna sighed. "What happened to Stan is so sad. I heard he was poisoned."

"It's true. I wish I knew who did it."

"I'm sure your mom and her department are all over it."

"Count on it, but—"

"Uh-oh. I know that tone. Nancy, you need to stay out of this case. Someone was murdered and not by accident, either."

"I know this isn't my normal kind of mystery to solve, but I can't do nothing while a killer runs free." A killer who was out to get her mother.

"Then pray the authorities find him fast. This is one mystery you need to stay away from."

"Now you sound like Carter."

Anna's laugh bubbled. "Sorry. Back to the look Carter had on his face. Tell me more."

"Laura and her daughter were there, and he was talking with Clair. Then right before he left, he regarded me over his shoulder with…that look." She'd been pondering it since, and the only thing she could come up with was he wanted his own child. His teenage nephew would be graduating this coming school year and heading off to college, so the timing was fine, but she wasn't sure she wanted to have kids. She liked things the way they were, and if she was to become a mother, her time would no longer be her own—she'd be caring for her little one. Helping solve crimes would become next to impossible between her full-time job at the library and a child. How had they not had this conversation before they married?

"What do you think his look meant?" Anna asked.

"I'm not sure, then again, I think I might know."

"Ask him. You need to communicate honestly and not guess at what each other is thinking. That's how misunderstandings happen."

"You are wise beyond your years."

"Ha. I'm plenty old enough to have common

sense. Speaking of which, you need to know there are some folks in town suggesting the sheriff knocked off Stan to kill the competition for her job."

"That's absurd." The people in Tipton County knew better. How could any of them think her mother capable of murder?

"I agree, but I thought you should know. They believe since she gave Stan the first tray...well you get the picture."

"I do, but it's ridiculous."

"I'm so thankful your mom didn't eat those pies."

Nancy blinked back sudden tears as the gravity of how close Mom had come to death hit her. She needed to figure out who wanted Mom dead. She simply wouldn't let anyone know what she was up to. How dangerous could it be if no one knew?

Lyle combed through old cases Mary had handled. The murderer was likely someone out for revenge—someone who had recently been released from prison. He'd follow up on two men who had been brought up on drug charges who'd been released within the past month.

He remembered the duo well. They'd been caught dealing near the high school and had refused to flip on their boss. Mary decided to use them as an example and pushed to have them prosecuted to the fullest extent of the law.

A shadow crossed his desk in the bullpen. He looked up and grinned. "I might have a lead on who tried to kill you."

Mary raised a brow.

He turned his computer screen for her to see. "They were let out three weeks ago. Plenty of time to plot your demise."

"I need to grab something from my office and then we can go pay them a visit." She strode to her office.

He shook his head, went after her, and closed the door. "Maybe you should sit this one out. Let Carter and me handle it."

She looked at him as if he had two heads. "You know me better than that."

He did, but that wouldn't stop him from trying to talk sense into her. "If this was Nancy, what would you tell her?"

"It's too dangerous and to let the authorities handle it." She leveled a look that brooked no argument. "I am the law, so don't try and talk me out of this."

He needed to tread carefully. Mary was as stubborn and bullheaded as her daughter. "Yes, you are. But you have the election to think about and a department to run. Let us do our jobs." He didn't want to point out she was too close to the situation to be objective. It would do no good, but it was a valid argument nonetheless.

Mary stared past him for a moment as if contemplating his words. "You make a good point. I have a lot going on, and I don't want to jeopardize the safety of anyone in Tipton County by diverting all my time and energy to trying to find the killer when I have two highly trained deputies more than capable of doing the job."

He stood a little taller and pulled back his shoulders. "Thank you. I appreciate that. So we're agreed? Carter and I will handle the murder investigation."

She gave a quick nod then sat behind her desk. Her gaze locked onto his. "Keep Nancy out of this. I know my daughter, and I suspect she will be up to her eyebrows with this investigation if the two of you slip any information to her."

"Understood." He cared too much about both women to allow that to happen, and surely Carter would want to protect his wife. "I don't think you need to worry."

"You underestimate my daughter."

He blew out a breath. "I'll talk to Carter." He turned to leave.

"Wait."

He stopped and faced her.

"I asked Carter to run against me for sheriff."

"I heard. Did he file?" He still didn't understand her reason for wanting the competition. To his way of thinking it was the last thing she needed right now.

"I don't know. He needed to talk with Nancy. But if he does, I suspect my days here are numbered."

"Why'd you do it then?"

"Stan's death rattled me. Given a little time and space, I might not have made the same decision, but what's done is done. Besides, retirement sounds good."

"You hadn't even considered it before. Why the sudden change?"

"This case. It's caused me to do some soul searching. I'm not saying I'm ready to hang up my belt, but I'm open to the idea."

He nodded in understanding. "You're only fifty-five. What will you do?"

A flash of annoyance crossed her face then cleared. "I haven't lost yet. You don't have much faith in me."

He blew out a breath. "I have complete faith in you. It's the voters I don't have faith in. They're fickle."

The line on her forehead deepened. "Keep me in the loop on your investigation."

"You got it." He pulled open the door and strode to his desk. He and Carter had a lot to discuss.

Chapter Four

MARY SPOTTED NANCY POWER WALKING ALONGSIDE Anna and her little dog Freddy. She tapped her horn and waved. At least Nancy wasn't up to mischief. Had she made the right decision asking her son-in-law to run against her? She checked before leaving the county courthouse building where the sheriff's department was housed and learned he had filed.

Sadness filled her. She loved her job, but all good things ended at some point. She gripped the steering wheel tight. She was a realist and strongly suspected her time as sheriff was coming to an end. This wasn't the way she wanted to go out—losing an election. Not that she had lost it, but there was a chance she wouldn't win.

She'd always thought she'd know when it was time to leave office and simply wouldn't run for reelection. Talk about being shortsighted. She hadn't even thought about retirement, figuring she'd know when the time was right. The time had never been right.

Carter would have a lot to learn should he win. He was an exceptional cop, but there was so much more to the job. Nancy would be an asset, considering her experience as the sheriff's daughter.

A car horn blared. She blinked and slammed on the brakes skidding to a stop at a four-way intersection. "Pay attention." She'd let her mind wander and almost blew through a four-way stop.

Her phone rang. She clicked the button on the steering wheel. "Sheriff Daley."

"This is Traci at dispatch. Your neighbor reported a break-in at your home. According to Kent Price, a masked intruder is still inside. Deputies are en route."

"I'm almost there. Thanks for the heads up. I'm one minute out." She jammed her foot down on the accelerator. "Make that thirty seconds." Mary disconnected the call.

She parked a few doors down from her house and assessed the situation. Kent sat in his usual spot on his front porch across the street from her house and down two doors. She frowned at the seventy-something year old man who ought to know to go inside and lock his doors. She secured her Glock then crept from her SUV over to her neighbor. "He still in there?"

"Haven't seen anyone leave."

"Okay. Go inside and stay out of sight."

He patted the rifle on his lap. "I can take care of myself."

Her eyes widened. How had she not noticed that before? "Just the same. I'd feel better if you'd go inside."

"And I'd feel better staying here. Seems to me, you're on your own. You need me."

"You're a civilian."

His chest puffed out. "I'll have you know I served in Vietnam."

She looked around. Where was her backup?

Deputy Jacobson pulled up behind her rig. She

breathed a little easier. "Looks like my backup has arrived. Stay here." She looked at him pointedly. "I don't want to accidentally shoot you."

He waved her away.

She grinned and shook her head then hustled over to where Brett Jacobson stood. "You ready?"

"Let's do this."

"You cover the back in case he makes a run for it," she ordered.

They jogged across the street, and using shrubs for cover, they worked their way onto her property. Brett motioned that he was going around back. Mary plastered herself against the wall beside her front door, which stood ajar. Her heart beat wildly. *Lord, please keep us safe.* With her Glock between her hands she breached the door. Careful to avoid the creaks in the floor she cleared the front room, then the kitchen, bathroom, and guestroom. That only left her bedroom. She slowed and eased into her sanctuary. "I know you're in here. Surrender with your hands up where I can see them."

A noise in her walk-in closet sounded. "This is Sheriff Daley. Come out now!" She leveled her weapon at the closet entrance. She edged closer. Silence filled the house. *The window.* She yanked open the closet door and spotted the open window. She rushed to it and looked out. Where had he gone?

"Jacobson," she shouted.

The deputy came around from the back of the house to the side window. "He didn't come my way."

"That's because he escaped through this side window."

"Oh."

"Don't stand there. Go after him." Mary waved her arms shooing him away.

Brett sprinted out of sight.

Lyle ran a hand over his close-cropped hair as he interviewed Kent Price. "Can you describe the person you saw enter the sheriff's home?"

Kent rubbed the fuzz on his cheek. "My eyes aren't what they once were, but I'd say your man is a few inches shy of five-eight with a small build. He's a fast runner too. I saw him dart from the house, but he ran in the opposite direction of me."

Lyle studied the older man. Though in good shape for a man in his seventies, there was no way he would have been able to chase the burglar. "What else can you tell me?"

"He wore jeans, a black hoodie, and dark sunglasses. I'm guessing he was under forty based on how fast he ran."

Well past forty, Lyle kept in shape by lifting weights and running, so Kent's guess could very well be wrong. He pulled out his card and handed it to the man. "If you think of anything else please call me."

"I can let the sheriff know if I think of something."

"That'd be fine, but I'd still like to hear from you directly."

"Sure thing, Deputy. I should've known that man was up to no good. Especially with being so overdressed for the weather."

"Why's that?"

"He was shifty. He looked around more than the average person."

"Did you see his face? You sound confident you saw a man. Did he have any facial hair?"

"Well, now that you mention it, I couldn't swear that it was a man, but it was a general sense."

Lyle nodded. "Okay. You have my card. Take care of yourself." He stepped down the stairs and headed across the street to Mary's home which had several cars parked along the curb. Nancy's Mustang still shone in the dimming light of an incredibly long day. He knocked on the front door, which swung wide, almost before he removed his hand.

"Lyle." Nancy reached out and pulled him inside. "What did Mr. Price say?"

"He didn't give me much to go on."

The hopeful look in Nancy's eyes faded. "Oh."

"How's your mom?"

"Angry enough to spit nails. Carter is with her in the kitchen."

He nodded and headed that way. He paused before entering the open space. Mary and Carter sat at the table, talking in hushed tones—probably to keep what they were saying away from Nancy.

Even seated, Mary was a force to be reckoned with. Her strong and sturdy build gave him confidence she could take care of herself in any situation, but he wanted to protect her more than anything right now. To do that he needed to find who was behind the murder, and now the break-in. Were the two cases related or simply a coincidence?

He cleared his throat to alert them to his presence then strode over to the table. He pulled out a chair and sat beside Carter.

"What do you know?" Mary looked at him

expectantly with brown eyes the shade of chocolate pudding, his favorite dessert.

His stomach growled. "Your neighbor is observant but says his vision isn't great. He believes the person who broke in was a man but never actually saw his face, other than to note he wore sunglasses."

Carter pushed his chair back and stood. "It's been a long day. I'm going to head home." His focus landed on his mother-in-law. "If you need anything call."

She nodded. "I'll be fine. Take good care of my daughter."

"Always." Carter squeezed her shoulder then left.

Nancy popped into the kitchen. "We're leaving, but you know we're close if you need anything."

"I know. Go home and stop worrying."

"I'm not worried."

"No? Then why do you have a chocolate ring around your lips?"

Nancy's hand shot to her mouth, and she wiped the chocolate away. "I was hungry."

Lyle hid a grin behind his hand. Nancy's love of dark chocolate was well known among her family and friends.

"See you later." Nancy stepped all the way into the room. She hugged her mom, met Lyle's eyes, then left. A moment later the front door clicked closed.

Lyle stood. "Be right back." He quickly locked the door then returned to the kitchen where his strong and capable boss looked incredibly vulnerable—she needed a friend not a deputy. "I haven't had a chance to eat, and I'm starving. Want to get dinner with me at Daisy's Diner?"

Her face brightened ever so slightly. "Sounds good. I've never had a bad meal there. Besides, I'm too tired to cook."

"Same."

"You cook?" Surprise gave her voice an uncustomary lilt.

"I have to eat, don't I?" He frowned. "Granted most of my food comes in the form of a frozen meal that I have to heat, or I go out."

She chuckled. "That sounds more like it." She grabbed a sweater and her purse then they headed out.

"Mind if I drive?" He asked.

"Not at all. I'm too distracted to be safe behind the wheel. I almost blew through a four-way stop earlier."

Shock reverberated through him. "Want me to pick you up on my way in tomorrow?" Mary was a conscientious driver. Clearly, the recent events surrounding her life had her rattled and distracted. Another reason she didn't belong investigating Stan's murder.

"No. Though I appreciate the offer, I can't show any sign of weakness. Besides, all I need is a good night's sleep."

"Carpooling with a coworker is not a sign of weakness." His grip tightened on the old Ford pickup's steering wheel.

"It is if you're the sheriff."

He shook his head at how ludicrous her statement sounded as he pulled to a stop along the curb in front of Daisy's Diner. He got out and met Mary on the sidewalk. Several couples strolled down the main drag of Tipton. He breathed in deeply the scent of home cooking coming from the diner. "My mouth is watering."

"Mine too. If they still have the roast, that's what I'm getting. Comfort food at its best."

"Mmm. Sounds good to me too." He pulled open the door, allowing her to enter ahead of him.

Mary headed toward the back. She greeted a few patrons along the way before sitting at a table that gave them both a clear view of the entire space as well as the entrance.

Kari, a long-time waitress at the diner, approached with a notepad. "Hi there, Sheriff. I heard about what happened last weekend. Poor Stan." She shook her head. "I'm so glad I wasn't there. Rumor is some of the witnesses are having nightmares."

Lyle cleared his throat. "That's unfortunate. It's really sad what happened, but we'll find whoever is responsible."

"Good. Makes me a little uneasy to eat anything I didn't prepare myself. You know?" She laughed nervously. "May I take your order?"

Mary handed back their menus. "We'd like two orders of the roast beef special if there's any left."

"There is." She scribbled their order on the notepad and walked away.

"I'm glad that's become a nightly special," Mary said.

Lyle nodded. It was nice to have a normal conversation that didn't involve talking about murder or some other crime. He glanced at Mary who had suddenly turned pale. "What's wrong?"

"Nothing...I..." She blew out a breath. "It's silly. I

let my imagination get the best of me and was suddenly afraid someone might poison my meal here."

If Kari hadn't been their waitress and Daisy the cook, he might feel the same, but he trusted both of them. Had he misplaced his trust? No. They were good to their core. "That's an understandable fear, but you don't need to worry. The chance of Daisy allowing someone near our food is nil. Besides that, I doubt our killer will strike the same way twice."

He didn't think it was possible, but her face had grown even paler. "Mary, look at me." Her eyes shifted to meet his. Fear and anger converged in her gaze. Mary was never one to be afraid. What was different this time? It wasn't like she'd never faced danger.

He reached an arm across the table palm up. "Give me your hand please."

Her brow wrinkled, but she did as he asked. Her touch sent a zip of electricity through him. *Whoa.* He wrapped his fingers around her cold hand. "Listen to me. No matter what, your friends and staff have your back. We will do everything in our power to make sure no one else dies, and we *will* find out who killed Stan. Do you hear me?"

She nodded and tugged her hand free, placing it in her lap. "I know, and I appreciate it. I'm sorry for letting my imagination get the better of me."

"It happens. Contrary to popular belief you're a normal human."

"Oh? People don't think I'm human?" A twinkle lit her eyes this time.

"Those of us who work for you have long suspected you're super human." He grinned.

"I'll take that, but you're right, I'm a mere mortal. I'm thankful for my faith in God. I turned this over to Him, and I need to leave it with Him and stop trying to take it back."

"Spoken like a woman of wisdom." His estimation of her raised another notch. "I haven't had a chance to tell you yet, but I talked with the parole officers about the two men we spoke of earlier."

She leaned forward slightly. "And?"

"They have alibis. They were working litter patrol."

"On a Saturday?"

He nodded. He'd thought it odd too, but since they were working off community service hours with a non-profit it made more sense.

Kari approached holding a plate of roast beef, mashed potatoes, and green beans in each hand. "Here you go. And don't you worry, Sheriff. I personally oversaw your meal. It's safe."

"Wow," Mary said. "That was really nice of you."

She shrugged. "If the situation was reversed, I'd hope someone would watch out for me too. Enjoy." She walked away.

Mary picked up her fork. "Here goes nothing. If I die, your number one suspect should be Kari."

He chuckled. "I don't think we need to worry." He cut a piece of roast and popped it into his mouth.

"What are you thinking?" Mary savored a bite of mashed potatoes.

"I think I need to ditch my normal dinner and get takeout here. This is so good."

She nodded and took another bite.

They ate in silence until they were both finished.

Mary leaned against the seatback. "We need to do this more often. I can't remember when I last enjoyed a meal this much."

She'd had him over for family dinner many times at her place along with Carter and Nancy and couldn't imagine how this outranked those times. "What's so special about this meal?"

"I guess I'm appreciating the little things more than I used to. Good food that I didn't have to cook and time with a good friend is a treasure I'm thankful for."

He bit his cheek to keep himself from saying something stupid like, how he'd like to be so much more than her friend. Instead, "friendship is a treasure," popped out of his mouth.

"You okay, Lyle? You're looking a little uncomfortable." Panic filled her face. "Oh no. Were you poisoned?"

"No. I'm fine."

She reached out and rested her hand on his forearm. "Are you sure? No nausea or dizziness?"

"None. I'm okay. A little tired and worn out but not sick." Her concern touched him. He patted her hand. "I'm fine."

"Good. For a second I had a flash of Stan right before he collapsed. I was afraid..." She shook her head, effectively tossing away the unfinished sentence.

"How about we get out of here?" He left enough money to cover their meals along with a generous tip and stood.

"I can pay my own way." Mary opened her purse.

"I know. But you've been making me dinner for

years. It's about time I treat you to one. It's only fair."

She closed her purse and stood. "When you put it like that, how can I refuse? Thanks." She waved to Kari on the way out.

Lyle scanned the street and sidewalk for trouble as they walked to his pickup. Nothing appeared out of place, so why did the hair on the back of his neck stand up as soon as they'd left the diner?

Chapter Five

MORNING SUNLIGHT WARMED NANCY'S BACK AS she stood near Carter on the steps outside the library. She crossed her arms. "How could you?"

"How could I not? Your mom *asked* me to run against her."

"I realize that, but I'm sure she didn't mean it." She shook her head and swallowed back threatening tears. She took a breath and let it out.

"You said to do what I thought was best."

She pressed her lips together. He was right—she hated being wrong. "You really think running against your mother-in-law is for the best?"

"Honestly, I have no idea, but my gut said I should respect her request. I trust she knows her own heart and what she's doing."

Nancy frowned. "I suppose. How come you told me this right before I have to open the library instead of last night?"

"With the intruder at your mom's house, it slipped my mind. By the time I remembered, you were already asleep, and then I was out the door before you got up."

His shift started at six in the morning. She uncrossed her arms and stuffed a hand into her sweater pocket. "Okay. I understand. But I don't know who to campaign for." Maybe she should stay out of the election altogether.

His brows lifted. "Seems to me that should be obvious. Your man needs you."

She chuckled. "So does my mom." She placed a tender kiss on his cheek. "I love you."

"Love you too. Watch out for paper cuts." He winked.

"I'll do that. You watch your back." She hadn't worried about Carter being killed in the line of duty until Saturday. Now everything had changed—she hated change.

"Always." He pulled her close and soundly kissed her. "Now it's a good day. Want to grab lunch together?"

"Text me when you get a break, and I'll let you know if I'm free. It depends on Laura and how busy we are."

Carter nodded. "See you later." He turned and strode to his vehicle.

Nancy opened the library and set about her normal tasks. Her mom and Carter were up for the same job. If Mom won the election, Carter still had a job, but if Cater won, Mom would be out of work. Was she prepared for that? Had she been setting aside a nest egg? They never talked money so she had no idea.

She'd not thought to worry about her mom in the past. Mom had always been so capable and seemingly invincible, but the other night after the break-in, she had looked vulnerable sitting at her kitchen table. It had come as a shock to realize her mother was only human. Maybe now *was* a good time for Mom to retire.

The answer to her question about who to

campaign for became clear. She'd support them both. No one would blame her. Besides, God was in control, and nothing she did or didn't do would change that.

Now to figure out who wanted her mom dead. If only she had someone to bounce ideas off of. In the past she had Carter or Anna, but this time she didn't dare let anyone know what she was up to.

Nancy busied herself with checking in books then adding them to the cart to be shelved. Laura would be there in an hour, and she wanted to have these ready when she arrived.

A woman and her young son walked inside and made a direct path to the children's section. She watched for a moment as he reached for a displayed book then plopped onto a red beanbag chair and opened it. His mom headed for the fiction section.

Nancy pulled her focus back to the task at hand, and before it seemed possible, Laura breezed into the library.

"Good morning." Laura dropped her purse into the bottom drawer of the circulation desk. "How's it going so far today?"

"It's been an average morning."

"So no excitement here, huh? Count yourself lucky. There's a horrible accident on Main Street."

"Oh, no. What happened?"

"From what I was able to gather, someone had a medical emergency and accelerated through town until she started smashing into cars on Main Street. After hitting six parked cars she finally came to a stop."

"Wow. Was anyone hurt?"

"I don't know. It's a mess though."

Alarm struck her. "I parked my car on Main."

"Your Mustang is fine. This happened over by Roaster's Coffee."

"Thanks for the info. I'm going to take a break and check on a friend." She grabbed her phone and rushed outside. If she hurried, she could check on Pepper, find out what happened, and get back in fifteen minutes.

Nancy two-timed it along Main. Laura wasn't exaggerating. The first and second cars in the lineup looked totaled. Who had been behind the wheel? She pushed inside Roaster's. A hum of activity filled the familiar shop. She spotted Pepper at the counter. "Hey. Any idea who caused the mess outside?"

Pepper's sympathetic gaze met hers. "No one told you?"

"Told me what?"

"It was your mom, Nancy." She filled a paper cup with coffee and popped on the lid.

A wave of dizziness gripped Nancy. "What happened?"

"I don't know. I heard she had a medical emergency and was unconscious behind the wheel. They took her to the hospital in Salem."

The dizziness passed. "Thanks. I'll call you later." She turned.

"Hey."

Nancy shifted back to face her friend. "What?"

Pepper came around the counter holding a white bag and a coffee. "For the road. I figured you'd be here sooner or later and made you a bagel with cream cheese. The coffee is black. Just the way you like it."

"What did I do to deserve a friend like you?

Thanks." She took the meal and rushed out. She scanned the authorities processing the scene and spotted Carter across the way. She hustled over to him. "What's the deal with not calling me?"

"I haven't had a chance. Lyle went with your mom to the hospital."

"Is she going to be okay?"

"The medics were uncertain. I'm sorry for not calling or texting, but this literally happened a half hour ago and there hasn't been time. Someone was in one of the cars she hit."

Nancy's heart pounded. "Who?"

He checked his notebook that was always with him. "A Gail Stephenson."

"Never heard of her. Is she okay?"

"She seemed shaken up, but other than that she'll probably only be sore. Are you going to the hospital to see your mom?"

"I..." Could she? Laura would need to pick up her daughter in the afternoon. Did she have time? "I'm not sure. I'll need to check. I'll text if I can get away."

He nodded then returned to whatever he was doing when she interrupted. It looked like he was measuring the skid marks of a parked car.

Nancy strode back to the library, placed the food at her desk, then walked the stacks in search of Laura. She didn't have far to look since she was only a row away from the circulation desk. "My mom was the driver."

Laura gasped. "I had no idea. Is she okay?"

"I don't know. She was taken to the hospital in Salem. Can you manage things here for a couple of hours so I can go and see her?"

"Of course. Don't you have a volunteer coming in later?"

"I do. Which is great timing. I'll be back before you need to pick up Clair."

"If anything changes, let me know, and I'll get someone to bring her here so I don't have to leave."

"You can do that?"

She nodded. "My neighbor has offered to help in a pinch."

"Cool. I'll text as soon as I know something." She grabbed all her stuff and headed out. This simply didn't make sense. Mom was a good driver and in perfect health, at least as far as she knew. Had she been keeping something from her or had the killer done something to sabotage her? No, it couldn't have been the killer. They said Mom had a medical emergency.

She eased behind the wheel of her Mustang, tucked the cup between her legs since her classic car didn't have cup holders, and set the rest of her stuff on the passenger seat. She ate the bagel as she drove, even though she wasn't hungry. With no idea what she would walk into at the hospital, she didn't want to have to take time out to eat later.

About thirty minutes later, she parked in the garage at Salem Hospital and went into the emergency department. She approached a woman standing in the middle of the waiting area who appeared to be a hospital employee. "My mom was taken here by ambulance not long ago."

The woman's face softened. She held a tablet. "What's her name?"

"Mary Daley."

"I see her here. I'll buzz you back and let the charge nurse know who you are."

"Thank you." She hurried over to the doors, which opened when she approached, then walked toward the nurse's station in the center.

A woman with kind brown eyes directed her gaze at her. "You must be Nancy. I'm Mandy. You look a lot like your mom."

"You know my mom?"

"We met a few minutes ago. She told me all about you and to expect you."

Relief washed over Nancy. Mom was okay if she was talking. She walked beside the nurse to a rather large room and went inside. Her mother lay on the bed covered with a white sheet and thin blanket. "Mom." She rushed to her side and rested a hand on her shoulder. Her throat thickened, seeing her mom like this. Bruising was already visible on her face, she had a bandage beside her left eye, and she looked so incredibly tired.

"It's about time you showed up. I've been here at least twenty minutes."

Nancy chuckled then coughed to cover the tears that threatened. "Sorry for taking so long. No one called to tell me what happened. I had to discover it on my own."

"Ah. Then I'm impressed."

Nancy looked around the room. "I heard Lyle came with you. Where'd he go?"

"Right here." Lyle strode into the room. "Had to make a call." He stepped to the other side of the bed.

A nurse came in carrying a kit of some sort. "We need to take blood." She checked Mom's wrist bracelet against her blood draw order. Apparently satisfied she had the right patient, she got down to business. Nancy moved away to stand beside Lyle. She kept her voice low. "They're checking for drugs?"

"Among other things."

"I can still hear you both." Mom frowned as the needle was poked into her vein.

"Can you tell me how you were feeling before you lost consciousness?" Lyle held a pen and notepad.

"A little woozy, but I certainly didn't feel faint. Do you really think I was drugged?"

"At this point, anything is possible. Until your labs come back, we only have questions." Lyle tucked his notepad into his pocket.

Nancy's gaze slid to the machine tracking her mom's heartbeats and blood pressure, which looked high to Nancy's way of thinking. "Have you seen a doctor yet?"

"When I first got here. She ordered tests. Someone will be coming to take me to radiology."

"Good. We need to figure this out." Nancy couldn't believe her mom's medical emergency was due to natural causes.

"The sooner the better," Lyle added.

He wasn't fooling her, pretending to be here officially. Anyone with eyes could see he cared for her mom.

"I'm going to find out what's going on. Be right back." Nancy turned to leave and jumped when the alarm on the machine monitoring her mom went off. She whipped back around and panic rose inside her. "Mom."

Chapter Six

LYLE LEANED FORWARD IN THE WAITING room and rested his head in his hands. Mary had been rushed off to surgery after having a massive heart attack. Fear consumed him. What if she didn't make it?

"Here you go." Nancy handed him coffee in a Starbucks cup.

He looked up. "Where'd this come from?"

"The gift shop sells Starbucks coffee."

He took off the lid and breathed in the rich coffee aroma. He'd consumed more coffee in his life than he cared to admit, and mostly because he liked the smell and the caffeine, not because of the taste.

"Don't worry, I added cream and sugar." She sipped her own brew.

"Thanks." He popped the lid back on and simply held the cup, taking comfort in the warmth between his ice-cold fingers. "It shouldn't be too much longer." He said as much for Nancy as himself.

She cradled her cup and stretched her legs forward. "I called Carter and let him know what's going on. He said he's praying."

"Good." What would he do if Mary didn't make it? Morning had never been his favorite time of day, but she always made it better, even her sometimes gruff ways could put a smile on his face. He loved her strength and no nonsense take on life.

"Anyone ever tell you, you're a man of few

words?"

He titled his head to the side. "I might have heard that before." He offered a weak grin.

Mary's heart doctor, a woman who looked to be in her forties, approached them.

They both stood. "How is she?" Nancy asked.

"We found a blockage in her left artery and there was some damage to her heart."

Lyle's thoughts raced. She'd had a real heart attack—not one brought on by some drug. The doctor said something about a stent and went on to say she should make a full recovery.

"Your mom is a lucky lady," the doctor said. "If she hadn't been here when that heart attack struck, she'd probably be dead."

A shudder shook Lyle. He'd come so close to losing her.

"What about her car crash?" Nancy asked. "Any injuries from that?"

"She has some bruising as you know, but no evidence of internal bleeding or broken bones was noted—a miracle based on what I was told about the accident. We're waiting on the test results to help determine why she passed out."

"Doctor, someone tried to kill Mary this past weekend, and there was a break-in at her home last night. Do you think she could have been given something that made her dizzy enough to lose consciousness."

Surprise covered the doctor's face. "There are certainly drugs that could do that. I'll make sure to check for those. In the meantime, she should be awake soon. Once she's settled in a room you can see her. Normally, I'd release her, but considering the trauma her body has experienced today, a night or two in the hospital is advisable."

"Thank you," Lyle said.

They spoke with the doctor until she was paged and had to leave.

Nancy turned to him. "I don't know how to feel right now. The idea that Mom had a clogged artery is really scary. I thought she was in perfect health."

He nodded. His feelings were mixed as well. He patted her back. "Me too. Let's be thankful she's alive and worry about finding whoever tried to kill her on Saturday later."

Nancy's eyes widened. "That almost sounded like you're going to let me help."

"Your mom asked me to keep you out of it." He rubbed his chin. He couldn't believe what he was considering. Was it a mistake? He didn't want to put Nancy in harm's way, but they needed her—Mary's life was at stake. "You're good at ferreting out trouble, though your mom would never forgive me if anything happened to you."

"Don't forget Carter."

He nodded, although if he knew Carter, the man had kept his wife up to date about the case. "Him too." Lyle had given Nancy grief in the past about sticking her nose in police business when it put her life in danger, but this time her help might be essential and dare he say, worth the risk. He had no doubt whoever was behind the poison wouldn't hesitate to take out Nancy if she got too close, so they had to tread very carefully.

Nancy power walked beside Anna. "I've never been so afraid in my life. When that alarm went off in my mom's hospital room today, I thought for sure she was dead." Her voice shook.

"But she's not." Anna stopped to let Freddy sniff the ground. They walked in place while he did his dog thing until he was ready to move on.

"I know. But now, more than ever, I'm worried about her. Not only is a killer on the loose, but my mom's health isn't great. What if something happens to her?" After all these years of her mother serving in law enforcement, the chance that she might not come home had never really hit her until Stan's death. "I can't let someone hurt her."

"She'll be safe in the hospital," Anna said. "How come you haven't asked me to help figure out who killed Stan?"

"You told me to stay out of it. Besides, I didn't want to put you in danger."

"It hasn't stopped you before." Anna grinned.

"This time is different." The break-in at Mom's place had to be connected. If Mom hadn't had a blocked artery, she'd think whoever had broken into the house had left something behind that caused her mother's medical crisis today. Hmm. The doctor hadn't ruled out foul play, only that Mom had a legit reason for the heart attack. What if something unnatural had caused her to crash earlier, and the stress of everything had incited the heart attack?

"Nancy?"

"Yes?"

"Have you heard a word I've been saying?"

Nancy glanced in her direction. "I'm sorry. My mind wandered. What did you say?"

"Nothing much—only that I want to help you find Stan's killer." She held up a hand. "And before you say it, I know I told you it's too dangerous and to stay out of it, but I've changed my mind."

"You don't think it's too dangerous anymore?" Nancy couldn't believe Anna would suggest such a thing.

"Oh, it's too dangerous, but I know you and have no doubt you're in this up to your nose. I want to help."

Nancy looked around to make sure no one was within hearing distance. "You're right, but I haven't had a chance to do anything yet. I could use someone to theorize with. Are you sure you want to get involved? This could get really dangerous."

"As far as I'm concerned it already is. There is a killer among us in Tipton, and that's compelling enough to move me past any fear I might have."

Mary opened her eyes and noted the darkness outside. How long had she slept? The dimly lit hospital room was the last place she wanted to be, but she simply didn't have the strength or energy right now to demand she be released. Between the long hours she'd been putting in, the abuse her body had taken from the accident, whatever drug she'd been given, and her heart attack, she was wiped out.

A noise from the corner of her room drew her attention. She blinked and focused on the shape in the chair. Was that Lyle? The man shouldn't be here. He should be home getting a good night's sleep so he could figure out who wanted her dead. Whoever it was almost got their wish today. A fact she was all too aware of thanks to her hurting body.

Lyle shifted and sat up. "Hey, there. You're awake." He stood and stretched then walked to the side of her bed.

"Unfortunately," she said wryly. "I was having the most wonderful dream."

He chuckled. "How're you feeling?"

"Like I was hit by a truck. I don't remember ever being this sore."

"I imagine not moving around all day hasn't helped either. Can I get you anything?"

He had to be one of the kindest men she'd ever known. "Water?"

"Coming right up." He picked up her water bottle and held the straw to her lips.

She raised her head and drew in a long drink then rested her head against the pillow. "Thanks. Now what are you still doing here? I thought I sent you and Nancy home hours ago."

"You did. She listened, I didn't. I'm not comfortable with you being here alone with a killer on the loose. You dying isn't an option to my way of thinking. Not sure I'd know what to do without you."

Her insides turned to mush. That had to be one of the nicest things any man had ever said to her, including her ex-husband. She reached out her arm that wasn't attached to the IV.

He grasped her hand. "You okay?"

"Define okay?" Maybe it was the painkiller, or

she'd finally let Nancy get inside her head, but seeing Lyle here right now left her wanting something she hadn't desired in a very long time—the love of a man.

He gave her hand a light squeeze. "As in I don't need to get a nurse."

"Then I'm okay."

"Whew. You had me concerned. I should go and let you sleep."

"I thought you were my bodyguard." She didn't want him to leave.

"I'll be right outside your door."

"That sounds miserable. If you're staying anyway, you might as well be comfortable. That chair you were reclined in didn't look too bad."

"It's not. Are you sure about me staying?"

Fatigue washed over her. She mumbled yes and gave in to sleep.

Sometime during the night, Lyle must have left, because when she opened her eyes to sunlight streaming in the following morning, she was alone. Disappointment tasted like a bitter pill.

The door to her room opened and a smiling nurse entered. "Good morning. How are you feeling today?"

Now how was she supposed to answer that? She felt rotten, but did she really want the truth? "I've felt better."

"I would imagine so." The nurse checked her hospital bracelet then handed over a tiny cup-like thing with a pill inside.

Mary shook her head and groaned. "Is this necessary?"

"Yes. You need to take a blood thinner."

Fear shot through Mary as the reality of her

future hit her like a Mack truck. This was not good. "I really don't like to take pills."

"Your life could depend on that pill."

Mary nodded then tossed the pill in her mouth and swallowed.

"Very good." The nurse smiled.

A knock on her door drew her attention. "Come in."

Lyle pushed inside. He wore street clothes rather than the uniform he'd had on yesterday.

"You went home."

"Long enough to shower and grab a bite to eat. How're you feeling?"

She glanced at the nurse who was recording something into her notebook. "Alive."

He chuckled. "Alive is good." He plopped into the chair she'd spotted him in last night.

The nurse left and closed the door behind her.

"I didn't expect to see you today since you weren't here when I woke up."

"I promised Nancy I'd check on you. Any word on when you'll be released?"

"Not yet."

"Word of advice?"

She nodded.

"Don't rush leaving. Right now this is the safest place you can be. You're weak and you live alone."

"I'm well aware of my status, thank you very much." She was more than a little surprised Lyle was here rather than Nancy. Then again, Nancy had to open the library, although her assistant was quite competent.

A gleam lit Lyle's eyes. What was the man so

happy about? Okay, she was a bit grumpy today. She took a breath and let it out. Be kind. "Are you laughing at me?"

"Only on the inside."

She guffawed and instantly regretted it.

"Ha. I made you smile. When I walked in, that line on your forehead was so rutted I thought for a second I had the wrong room."

"You're a laugh a minute, mister."

"I try." His eyes still shone.

"Why are you really here, Lyle?"

He shrugged. "I needed to see for myself that you're okay. Plus your doctor asked me to stop in. The test results came back on your toxicology report. She should be by soon."

Disappointment washed over her, which was silly—and she wasn't silly. She and Lyle were coworkers and friends. There had never been anything more than that between them, and it was best for both of them if it stayed that way. Then again her career was all but over if the community lost confidence in her ability to serve. Maybe it wouldn't hurt to let him know she was interested. *Ack.* This was so unlike her. It had to be the trauma of everything addling her brain.

A rap on her door drew her attention as it opened.

"Good morning." Doctor Berry walked into the room and stopped at the edge of her bed. "I'm glad you're both here." Worry filled her face. "Valium was found in your blood. Do you have a prescription for that?"

Mary's stomach sank. This was getting more real by the second. "No."

"Then I suspect that is the reason you fell asleep behind the wheel. Whoever broke into your home probably anticipated what you'd eat or drink for breakfast and added several pills to it."

"But wouldn't she have known?" Lyle asked.

"Not necessarily. It would take about thirty minutes for the drug to take effect, and if she wasn't paying attention, she wouldn't have tasted it."

"I guess that explains why my morning coffee tasted off. I was in a rush and didn't have time to make a fresh pot."

Lyle looked at her. "How could that have happened? Wouldn't you have noticed pills in your coffee pot?"

"Yes, but if the pills were in the water reservoir, I never could have seen them."

The doctor nodded. "They would have dissolved in the water and mixed into the grounds as the coffee was made, assuming that's how you were drugged. I agree with your theory. It makes the most sense."

Lyle reached for his phone. "I'll make sure your coffee pot is tested and dusted for finger prints if it hasn't been already."

Mary nodded then turned her attention to Doctor Berry. "When will I be discharged?"

"I could set you free today, but I don't advise it. Your body has been through a trauma. I'd like to keep you here for observation until tomorrow. We'll see how things go today and reassess in the morning."

As much as she wanted to protest, Mary only nodded. Lazing the day away kind of appealed. Plus, if she was here one more day, Lyle wouldn't be as concerned for her safety as he would if she were home alone.

The doctor did a quick non-invasive exam then left the room. Mary tilted her head to face Lyle. "What's the plan?"

"Carter and I will follow up on a few leads then go from there."

"You have leads besides what the doctor told us?" That was news.

"They're probably nothing, but a few tips came in."

"Tell me about them."

"You should rest."

"Lyle," she used her boss tone.

He sighed and sat. "All right. We have video of the pie table from a citizen for about five minutes before the contest began. A couple of locals had pictures on their phones of people in the vicinity of the table. In addition, one of your other neighbors caught your intruder on his home surveillance, and we are still working on the mayor's email."

"They all sound promising. What can you tell me about the intruder?"

"Nothing yet." He stood and walked over to her bedside.

Her heartrate accelerated, and thanks to the blasted machine she was hooked up to, Lyle could see the effect he had on her. She cleared her throat. "I'll expect to be kept in the loop."

"You got it, boss." He reached out and lightly squeezed her hand then sauntered out.

She blew out a breath. Well, that was awkward.

Chapter Seven

Sitting behind his desk in the bullpen, Lyle replayed the surveillance video Mary's neighbor had emailed. It was next to impossible to know if he was looking at a man or a woman. The perpetrator's straight shape and gait could easily be a male or female. He ran a hand through his hair. They needed a break in this case, today, before Mary was released.

Carter slid a chair beside his. "It's a little grainy. Think you can clean it up a bit?"

"Maybe." Lyle ran the video through the Lightworks program on his computer. It helped, but the gender and identity of the person were still unclear. It'd be ideal to narrow down if they were looking for a man or a woman.

"Nice try." Carter stood. "There were no fingerprints on the coffee pot except the sheriff's."

"What about the footage from the fair? Anything useful on it?"

"Nothing obvious, but I thought I'd give it to Nancy to look over. She notices things most people don't."

Lyle's head shot up. "You sure you want to do that?" He was happy to have the extra set of eyes, and had planned to involve Nancy himself, but Mary wasn't his mother-in-law. She would be furious if she found out they involved her daughter in a murder investigation.

"No, but I don't know what else to do. I'm running out of leads."

"I hear you. I have an appointment with the mayor today. Maybe something new will be brought to light."

"I sure hope so because this person didn't give us much to go on."

"No one is perfect, Carter. Keep digging."

Lyle headed up the courthouse basement stairs where the sheriff's department was housed, to the mayor's office on the second floor. He pulled open the door and walked inside the tight reception room that led to a hallway. "Good afternoon, May. I'm surprised to see you here. I thought you worked at the post office."

"I do, but I help out here when Dad's usual receptionist is sick or on vacation."

"Your hours must be flexible."

She shrugged. "Not really, but I'm part time, so it usually works out for me to fill in. I actually fill in for businesses all over town, including the high school."

He noted her tired-looking eyes. Could she be pushing herself too hard? "I see. Good for you. I'm here to see your dad. He's expecting me."

The blonde-haired young woman stood. "If you don't mind, before you head back to see him, I have a theory about who poisoned the pies."

He stilled. "What's that?" More than likely this was a waste of time, but on the off chance it wasn't, he needed to hear what she had to say.

She lowered her voice. "Do you know Albert Dunnigan?"

He shook his head.

"Well, his wife has entered the pie baking contest every year for the past three years and always came in second. I think he deliberately sabotaged the pies so his wife wouldn't have to come in second this year."

"Sabotage and murder are very different. I don't think winning a pie-baking contest is motive for murder, but thanks for trying to help."

A small pout formed on her lips. "You're not even going to question him? I saw him near the table beforehand."

It might be worth talking to the man to see if he saw something no one else did. However, he hadn't noticed the man in any of the footage or any of the photographs. It was probably a wild goose chase, but if there was a chance Dunnigan saw something ... "I'll look him up. Thanks for the tip. Excuse me, May. I need to speak with your dad now."

"Of course. You know where his office is?"

"I do. Thanks." He strode past her desk and down the hall to the second door on the right then rapped on the doorjamb.

Charlie looked up from his desk and frowned. "Lyle." He shook his head and motioned for him to enter. "This murder business is horrible. How's the investigation coming along?"

"Slow but steady." As in steadily running out of leads and slow to discover anything new. "What can you tell me about Saturday? Did you notice anything or anyone unusual? Perhaps someone behaving oddly."

"I wish. I've wracked my brain. This event has been my purview since I've been in office. I personally know everyone who entered a pie, and I can't see any of them doing such a heinous thing." He clicked his tongue. "I really liked Stan. He was a good man and would've made an excellent sheriff."

Lyle narrowed his eyes. "Do you have a problem with the current one?"

"Don't put words in my mouth." He waved his hand. "I simply meant that this town could use a fresh face with new ideas."

The man had some nerve. "I imagine you're supporting Carter for sheriff then."

Charlie shifted in his oversized desk chair. "I am. He has big city experience and he has fit in well since moving to town. Being married to our favorite librarian is a bonus."

"Don't forget he's the son-in-law of our sheriff."

Charlie frowned. "How is she doing? I heard about what happened yesterday. She's in all of our thoughts and prayers."

"The sheriff won't be back at work for at least a week, but her doctor seemed optimistic. I'm sure she appreciates the prayer. She has a challenging road ahead of her."

The mayor's gaze drifted to his doorway then back to Lyle. "I'm thankful she's going to be okay. I'd hate to see any harm come to another one of our citizens."

Lyle glanced behind him to see if they had company—no one. He studied the mayor for a few seconds. He wasn't a huge fan of the man, but Charlie was generally okay and usually seemed sincere, except for right now. The man's face and voice lacked sincerity about Mary.

Mayor Charlie wouldn't have tried to poison Mary,

would he? From what Lyle observed, the man was decent and well liked. So why was he so anxious to get rid of the sheriff, and would he stoop to murder to ensure she was out of office?

"Deputy?" Charlie had a strained smile on his face. "Do you have any more information?"

"We were able to trace the email you received about the sheriff receiving the first batch of pies to judge to a burner phone. On top of that, the email account it was sent from was a dead end."

"A burner?" Charlie's forehead wrinkled.

"You know. A cheap phone that can't be traced."

"Oh, right. I knew that. This whole thing has me out of sorts."

Lyle tilted his head. "What I don't understand is if you didn't know who sent the instructions, why did you follow them?"

Charlie's face reddened. "I've asked myself that numerous times since, and I don't have an answer. I guess I was caught up in the excitement and didn't consider the fact it came from an email I didn't recognize."

"I see." He wasn't sure he believed the man, but why lie, unless he had something to do with the murder? He'd keep an eye on the mayor. If he had anything at all to do with Stan's death...he clenched his jaw to keep from grilling Charlie right now. Treading carefully would be wise. Making an enemy of the mayor would not be in his or the sheriff department's best interest.

Mayor Charlie cleared his throat. "So you're no closer to finding the murderer." He steepled his fingers. "Maybe we should bring in outside help. I know I don't need to tell you the person must be caught and fast. The townspeople are scared, and they have every right to be."

Why would Charlie want to bring in outside help if he was guilty? "Walk me through your day on Saturday." Lyle pulled out his voice recorder. He had a great memory, but this allowed him to observe the mayor as he spoke and have a recording of it to analyze later.

"It was a hectic day. Last year's winner backed out at the last minute. She was supposed to announce the winner."

"She didn't enter?"

Charlie shook his head. "She said she had enough blue ribbons, and it was time to give someone else a chance."

A noble woman, then again it could have been a ploy to get attention off of her. "What's this woman's name?"

"Lola Smith."

Lyle knew the name all too well. The woman was a nuisance. The sheriff had threatened to arrest her if she called 9-1-1 again for a frivolous reason. If memory served, she wanted to know the weather report the last time she'd called. The lonely, older woman still had plenty of life in her. When Mary had threatened to arrest her, Lola had let off a stream of curse words that rivaled some of the filthiest talk he'd ever heard. He added Lola to his growing list of suspects.

Nancy focused on the computer screen as it played

back the surveillance Mom's neighbors had captured on their security camera. She knew that walk, but couldn't place it. The person had a bounce in their step. Their heel barely touched the ground if it even did at all.

She squinted and leaned closer to the monitor. "Look at the shoes. They're white sneakers." She glanced over her shoulder at Carter. "Don't you think?"

"It seems so. White sneakers are pretty common."

"I know, but these are different." She paused the playback and used the tip of a pen to point. "See how the heel of the shoe is thicker in back than the average sneaker? I think we could be looking for a woman. That style was popular once upon a time."

Carter pulled her to standing and tugged her close. "You're the best." He kissed her soundly.

"Gross, Uncle Carter." Gavin walked into the room from the hallway. "Give a guy a break."

Carter held tight to Nancy. "If you had a girlfriend you wouldn't think this was gross." He planted another one on Nancy.

She giggled and pulled away. "Gavin, there's no rush to find a girl, and if kissing bothers you that much—"

Gavin raised a hand. "I was teasing. By the way, I have a date on Friday night."

Carter's brows rose when he looked at Nancy, but when he turned to face Gavin his face was impassive. "Who's the lucky lady?"

"A girl from school." He plopped onto the couch.

"Does she have a name?" Carter asked.

"Ciara. She's new in town and is friends with

Maddie."

"What about Maddie?" Nancy asked.

Gavin shot a look at her like she'd lost her mind. "She's not coming on my date. I'm a one woman at a time kind of guy."

Nancy held back a grin. "Glad to hear that. But won't she feel left out?" Nancy recalled Anna's words that Maddie and Gavin were the best of friends but had absolutely no romantic interest in one another. After Carter and Gavin moved into her house and she'd seen the two of them together on a regular basis, she had to agree, but it still seemed weird to think of him spending time with another girl. Gavin and Maddie had been inseparable since their sophomore year.

"No way. It was her idea." Gavin kicked off his shoes, stretched out on the couch, and pulled out his phone.

"Okay, but if things go beyond a single date, watch out for Maddie. She could begin to feel left out or like a third wheel."

Gavin held his phone between his hands, his thumbs poised for texting. "It's fine, Nancy."

Which was his way of saying stay out of it. She pressed her lips together. She probably shouldn't have said anything anyway. It was one date not a lifetime commitment.

Carter slipped his hand around hers and drew her back to the computer. "Does anything else stand out to you?"

"Not really. With that short cut she really looks like a man from the side."

"So we're looking for a shapeless woman with a

man's haircut and white sneakers that are a little higher in back than normal."

"It's not a man's cut. It's a pixie cut. On the right shaped face it's adorable." Nancy looked at the image again. "Whoever she is, she's smart. She seems to realize there's video surveillance." Not many women wore their hair that short around here. She ought to be easy enough to find if she lived in town.

Carter sighed. "I'm not convinced that's a woman."

"You were a minute ago."

"I know, but the heel could be an optical illusion."

Nancy frowned. He might be right. But if it was a man he was a small man. The person in the video was on the petite side. "How about posting this on social media with a 'have you seen this person caption?' Then leave the department's tip line number."

"That's genius. I'll get on that right now." He kissed her again then shooed her away from the computer.

Nancy picked up the murder mystery she was reading and snuggled into the recliner. "Read any good books lately, Gavin?"

"Always."

Gavin and Maddie led a book club at school. It had started their sophomore year, and they'd kept it going even through the summer. "Tell me about it."

"I'm actually talking to someone right now." He flipped his phone so she could see his texts.

"Okay." She opened her book and stared at the page, not seeing the words. Raising a teen who was practically an adult was a challenge, but all things considered, Gavin was a pretty good guy. He no longer snuck out at night like he had when they first moved to town, and he hadn't done anything too stupid for quite some time. Carter had definitely been a good influence on his nephew.

Technically he was now her nephew too, but it didn't feel like it. She'd come into his life too late. She cared about him and wanted great things for him, but he still treated her like his uncle's girlfriend—well, wife now.

Carter stood and headed toward the front door. "Be back soon."

He wore his work face. Nancy had no doubt he was headed to the sheriff's department.

"Okay. Be safe."

"Always." The door clicked closed behind him.

A few minutes later Gavin pocketed his phone. "Are you Uncle Carter's campaign manager?"

She looked up from the book. "Me?"

He gave her a look that asked, who else would I be talking to.

"Well, no. I only found out a short time ago he was running for office, and my mom is running against him." Surely he realized the difficult position she'd been put in.

"He's your husband. Shouldn't you support him?"

"Of course I will. But I will also support my mom. I'm Switzerland—neutral."

"All my friends' parents are going to vote for him. They said the sheriff is past her prime."

"Ouch." Her mom might be over fifty, but she wasn't that old.

"Just telling you what I've heard."

"I know, but your friends' parents are being ageist. It's not right."

"Right or wrong, it is what it is."

She puffed out a breath and stood. "I'm going to take a drive to Salem and visit my mom."

"I heard Uncle Carter say she was being released in the morning." Gavin's gaze bore into her. "Why not wait to see her when she gets home?"

"Sometimes a girl needs her mom." She grabbed her phone, keys, and purse.

"It's past visiting hours," Gavin said.

She glanced at the wall clock. How could it possibly be nine already? "I'll text your uncle and let him know where I went." She strode out and headed next door to Anna's. Hopefully her friend was home. She knocked and a moment later the door opened.

Anna stood there in shorts, a tank, and no makeup. "Nancy. Is everything okay?"

"You were headed to bed?"

"I was, but come in." She opened the door wider. "Quick, before Freddy realizes the door is open and makes a run for it. He went to bed an hour ago."

"I don't want to keep you. I know you have an early morning."

"It's fine. Have a seat. Would you like a cup of chamomile tea?"

"No thanks. I won't be long." She shot off a text to Carter, letting him know where she was.

"Why are you here, Nancy?" She asked with all the concern of a mother.

"Because I wanted to see my mom tonight and realized it's past visiting hours."

"So you came here instead?"

"You're the next best."

Sympathy filled Anna's face. "What's going on?"

"Everything is changing, and I don't like it."

"You're talking about the election?"

Nancy nodded. "Gavin suggested Carter will win the election based on what he's hearing people say at school."

"He might be right. With your mom's health what it is, it makes sense for her to change her lifestyle. Being sheriff has to come with a lot of stress, which can't be good for her heart."

"I suppose." Nancy agreed reluctantly. Maybe Carter taking over would be a good thing, except she knew the kind of hours her mom put in and didn't want that for Carter. "Do you think Carter would make a good sheriff?"

"I have no doubt." Anna studied her face. "Where's this coming from? I'd think you'd be happy for your husband."

"I should be." It hurt to have the town turn their back on her mom. "But I know how it will change our lives if he wins, and I'm not sure we're ready for that. We've been married less than a year."

Anna nodded. "And you're afraid you'll drift apart?"

"Something like that. I'll miss him."

Anna sighed. "How did you manage all these years with your mom being the sheriff?"

"I inserted myself into her life at work." Is that why she enjoyed solving mysteries so much?

"And you won't do that with Carter?" Anna shook her head. "Girl, you've been doing that since he came to town."

Nancy grinned sheepishly. "I suppose you're right."

"Oh, I know I am. What else are you worried about?"

"My mom. Someone wants her dead, and they are still at large. What if this turns into a cold case and the person is never found?"

"I doubt that will happen, but you have to remember who your faith is in. No matter what happens, Nancy, He is in charge. We have to trust Him."

"What if I don't like what He lets happen?"

Anna shrugged. "We both know that's a possibility. It's not like He is Santa Claus or a genie, granting our every wish. Life can get messy, as you well know, but God is there to help you wade through that mess."

Nancy opened her mouth but no sound came out. Everything her friend said was true. "Sometimes I wish you weren't so wise. I wanted to have a pity party, and you make it impossible."

Anna smiled. "I understand the desire for a pity party. I've been there, but I learned He is faithful."

Nancy nodded. "Guess I'd better get home and let you go to bed." She stood and hugged Anna. "Thanks for answering the door."

"Always for you."

Nancy headed home. What if the killer was someone she knew? She shivered in the warm evening air.

Chapter Eight

FLUSTERED DIDN'T BEGIN TO DESCRIBE HOW Mary felt, sitting beside Lyle as he drove her home from the hospital. She'd expected Nancy or even Carter to rescue her, but according to Lyle *he* wanted to pick her up, even though he was now doing her job as well as his own, since he was next in command.

They'd always had a special connection, but the past few days had been different. Her heart beat in what had to be an unhealthy fashion so soon after having a heart attack. She closed her eyes and breathed in and out, in and out. She needed to get it together.

"Are you feeling okay?" Lyle asked, concern tinging his voice.

Her eyes shot open. "All things considered I feel great." He didn't need to know she fantasized about a life with him—no one needed to know that, including Nancy. Her daughter had tried to push the two of them together more than once. But it could never work between them, not as long as she was Sheriff.

"Good. I have a surprise for you at your place."

She looked in his direction. He wore a white polo style T-shirt and khaki shorts with deck shoes. He looked as relaxed as she'd ever seen him and downright handsome. She couldn't think about Lyle like this. He was one of her deputies. "What kind of surprise?"

"If I told you, it'd ruin the surprise, but suffice it to say, it's doctor approved and I think you'll love it."

She nodded. "I'm not a fan of surprises. I look terrible."

"You look beautiful."

Her jaw hung open. How could he say that? Her face was black and blue and it had been days since she'd showered. Even though she managed to make her hair look decent, she felt ugly. "You shouldn't lie, Lyle."

"I'm not. You've been given a second chance at life. Don't ruin it."

She frowned. He was getting sentimental. How was she supposed to deal with this side of the man she'd come to rely on as her right-hand both professionally and now personally?

He chuckled.

"What's so funny?"

"You. It's driving you nuts to not be in control."

He had that right. "What's your point?"

"This detour might be a good thing for you."

"What detour?" She looked around and noted they were still on highway 22.

"Your health scare. An incident like this is a good time to take a step back and reassess."

The Lord knew she'd had plenty of time for that over the past couple of days. She was still torn about being or perhaps not being sheriff any longer. She'd known nothing but work since she was old enough to hold down a job, and the idea of not working was abhorrent. However, turning over the stress of being the sheriff had begun to appeal. "If I wasn't sheriff, what would I do?"

She sensed more than saw him look in her direction then back at the road. "You really want to consider the possibility of not winning?"

His surprise was reasonable, considering how ardent she had been about keeping her job. "Yes. I've had a lot of time on my hands while in the hospital, and aside from trying to figure out who is out to kill me, I also pondered life after law enforcement."

"And what'd you come up with?" he asked softly.

"This town could use a P.I."

"Excuse me? I can't believe you said that." He laughed. "Sorry, but do you really want to follow suspected spouse cheaters around to catch them in the act?"

"Of course not. I wouldn't take on cases like that."

"That's the bread and butter of a private investigator."

"It doesn't have to be. I could do something like Nancy does and consult."

"Nancy isn't paid."

"True." They had the budget to pay her daughter, but since she was an amateur, it didn't seem like a good use of the department's money. As her right hand man this was no secret to Lyle. "Maybe I could go around to schools and teach self defense."

"You might enjoy that. It sounds a whole lot better than being a private investigator." Lyle pulled up to her house and set the brake. "Home sweet home."

Hadn't he said something about a surprise? She got out.

Lyle moved to her side and crooked his arm toward her.

She slid hers through his. "This isn't necessary."

He shrugged. "Maybe not, but you're recovering from a lot. Your surprise is inside."

Lyle stayed at her side as she walked to her door then entered.

Welcome home.

Her eyes widened and cool air washed over them. Someone must have come over and opened her windows early this morning to get it this cold in here—maybe a bit too cool, but it was still nice. A *Welcome Home* banner hung in the entryway, and beyond it a vase filled with flowers sat on the kitchen counter. "How sweet. Did you do this?" A mouthwatering scent filled the house. She walked in further.

"Nancy helped. She cleaned your house and made enough meals to last you a week, so there's no need to do anything but rest. She also suggested a list of movies you wanted to see but never did." He motioned toward a short tower of movies on the coffee table. "And there's a stack of books from the library she thought you'd enjoy."

"This is...unexpected." Moved to tears, she blinked rapidly. No one had ever done anything like this for her. "I don't understand why the two of you went to so much trouble, but I sincerely appreciate it." The sunflower-filled vase was perfection and put a smile on her face. "Sunflowers are my favorite. How'd you know?"

Lyle shrugged. "Lucky guess. I'm glad you like them."

"I love them. Thank you." She took a breath and blew it out softly between her lips. This was a different side of Lyle. One she'd not seen before all her medical drama. She turned to face him and rested a hand on his forearm. "I'm going to be okay. You don't need to worry or pamper me."

He reached over and gently squeezed her hand that rested on his arm. "I know. The thing is, you've never been in a position that any of us felt we could do something to help you. You're an incredibly self-sufficient and strong woman. Let us pamper you for a bit." He grinned. "But don't get used to it."

She laughed softly. "Understood." Right now the only thing she wanted was a hot shower, her softest sweatpants, and a sweatshirt—this place was way too cold. "And thanks. If I can't do my job this is the next best thing." She walked him to the door. "Will you stop by tonight and give me an update on the murder investigation? You can come for dinner. If I know my daughter, she probably left way more food than I should eat."

"An offer I can't refuse. Promise me you're going to rest in the meantime?"

"You have my word." At least for today since her body wouldn't allow her to do anything else. She hoped to sneak back to work in the morning. Maybe if she arrived super early and kept the blinds closed, no one would notice her.

"If you need anything, text or call."

"I'll be fine. It looks like you and Nancy thought of everything."

"We tried." He turned and walked out into the warm sunshine.

Maybe laying outside in the sunny backyard was a better idea than this cold house.

Lyle's grip tightened on the steering wheel of the cruiser as he drove away from the local hair salon. He'd hoped the employees there might recognize the person in the still shot they'd made from the surveillance video. He left a copy of the photo there in case someone might happen in and recognize the person. Frustration consumed him. So far every tip the photograph had garnered had been a dead end. At this rate he'd have nothing promising to tell Mary tonight when he updated her about the case.

Carter had someone pulled over ahead. Lyle eased to a stop behind him, keeping an eye out for trouble. When the car drove away, Lyle got out and met Carter on the sidewalk. He updated him on his progress with the case.

The furrow on Carter's forehead deepened. "I was afraid of that."

"But it's the only place in town." Where else would the person go?

"Some people cut their own hair, or have a friend do it or even go to another town for a cut."

He should have thought of that. With everything that was going on with Mary, he wasn't himself.

"How's the sheriff?"

"Considering what she's been though she's amazing. But I could tell she was worn out. She got teary-eyed when she spotted the flowers."

Carter raised a brow. "You must be mistaken. She probably had something in her eye." He winked.

Lyle chuckled. They both respected and cared a lot for Mary, but she was a force to be reckoned with when she was healthy. "She appreciated everything Nancy did. I have a suspicion no one has ever pampered her like that."

"You could be right. Nancy says little about her dad, but I have the impression he wasn't the nurturing sort."

"No, he wasn't." Lyle had only met the man a couple of times before he abandoned Mary and Nancy, and he hadn't been impressed. The man was self centered and arrogant. What Mary saw in him he never understood.

"I forgot you've been in their lives for so long."

He nodded. Mary and Nancy were like family. He'd always thought of Nancy like a daughter. Had spent many hours on his days off entertaining her when she was little so Mary could have a couple of hours to herself.

"Mind if I ask you something?" Carter had an uneasy look on his face.

Lyle's gut tightened. "Long as you don't mind me not answering."

"Fair enough." He rubbed the back of his neck. "How come you and the sheriff never got together?"

"She's the sheriff."

"That's the only reason?" Shock filled Carter's voice.

"It is from my perspective."

"Hmm. Well, here's the thing. Nancy is convinced that you and her mom belong together. She's only gotten more insistent since the sheriff's heart attack. Would you consider asking her out if she loses the election?"

"Why do you do that?" He was done with this

topic. At least for now.

"Do what?" Carter tilted his head slightly.

"Call her the sheriff all the time. She's your mother-in-law."

"I know, but I can't call her Mom, and calling her Mary feels weird. How do you call her Mary?"

"We've been friends a long time."

Carter didn't look convinced that was all there was to it, but he dropped the subject. He turned and called over his shoulder as he walked away, "Don't think I didn't notice you dodged my question."

Lyle grinned and shook his head. Nancy had married well. This town would be in good hands should Carter win the election.

"Excuse me." A woman who looked to be in her thirties waved and called out to him as she quickly walked in his direction.

He looked around to see if perhaps she'd waved to someone else—no one. He squared his shoulders and faced the woman when she stopped a couple feet away. "Is there something I can help you with, Ma'am?" She had a bruise on her forehead that she'd tried to cover with makeup, but to him it was as clear as the freckles on her nose.

"I'm Gail Stevenson. The sheriff struck my car the other day."

His body tensed. "How are you doing?"

"Other than a few bruises and a sore neck I'm fine. I was actually at the hair salon under the drier when you were there a bit ago showing that photo. After you left I asked to see the copy."

"Did you recognize the person?"

She shook her head. "No, but I did recognize the

wig. It used to be mine."

Wig? "Come again?"

"I'm a cancer survivor." She looked the picture of health.

"So you're sure it's your wig? The picture wasn't super clear." Could this be the break they'd been searching for?

"I'd know that wig anywhere."

Excitement rippled through him.

"I wore that thing for a long time. It always parted in the most annoying spot and..." she pulled the photo he'd left at the salon out of her purse and pointed. "See that. I never could get it to cooperate right there."

Sure enough, the wig rose up in one spot. He hadn't thought anything of it before, but knowing it was a wig put an entirely new light on things. "Do you recall who you sold the wig to?"

She grinned and handed him a scrap of paper.

He took the scrap. "Erika." He turned the paper over. "That's it? No last name or phone number?"

"No, but at least you know you're looking for someone named Erika."

He tucked the paper into his pocket. "Thanks for your help."

"Sure thing. I like the sheriff. I'm sorry someone is trying to hurt her, and I'm extra sorry I got caught in the middle."

"Quite literally," he mumbled.

She chuckled. "Please tell her I'm praying for her."

"I will. I know she'll appreciate your prayers. One more question if you don't mind."

"Sure."

"Is the person in the picture the woman you sold the wig to?"

She frowned. "I'm not sure. The woman I sold it to was meatier, but a body can change."

"So you believe the person in the photo is a woman?"

She tilted her head. "You don't?"

He cleared his throat. "Thanks again for the tip." He waited for her to walk away before returning to the cruiser.

They finally had what looked to be a solid lead. But would it be too little too late?

Chapter Nine

Nancy fluffed the pillow behind her mom's back.

"Nancy, please stop fussing over me." She looked exasperated.

Nancy sat on the coffee table directly in front of the sofa. "I'm sorry. I didn't mean to upset you."

"I'm not upset, but I'm also capable of adjusting my own pillow. I appreciate that you want to help, but maybe stick to things I can't do right now."

"Okay. That's probably for the best." Mom wasn't supposed to lift anything over five pounds so that left a lot for Nancy to help with. "Any news on the murder investigation?"

"Nothing yet. Lyle said he'd stop by for dinner and update me." She frowned as she stared at the wall clock.

"It's only six-fifteen. I'm sure he'll be here any minute."

A rap on the door echoed through the house.

"See. I bet that's him now." Nancy stood.

"Just the same, check the peephole before you open the door."

Nancy looked through the hole then grinned. "It's Lyle," she said over her shoulder. She unlocked and opened the door wide for her second favorite law enforcement man. "Hi. Mom said you were stopping by. Dinner is in the oven and should come out in five minutes."

"Did you make enough for two?"

"Depends on how hungry you are. She neglected to tell me you were coming over until a moment ago."

He chuckled. "Okay. I have a lead on the case. Why not throw in another serving and hang out for a couple minutes."

"Really? You're willingly sharing information with me? And in front of my mom?"

"It only seems fair since you're feeding me, and I think your mom will agree to me sharing this information with you."

She placed the back of her hand on his forehead. "Are you feeling okay?"

He laughed and brushed her hand aside. "I want this person caught, and you're good at following the clues."

"So are you. I know my mom, and she won't like you telling me anything."

"Too bad. We need all the help we can get."

She'd never known Lyle to be insecure. What had happened to cause his self-doubt? Or maybe it wasn't self-doubt but rather determination to protect her mom even with the help of an amateur sleuth.

"I'm sure I could catch this person on my own, but time is of the essence."

She nodded. Though her mom was a trained professional, she was weak and vulnerable right now. Living alone wasn't the best situation for her, but Mom refused to come stay with her and Carter. Stubborn woman. She'd be so much safer at their place.

Lyle made his way to the living room and explained about his lead. Shock of all shocks, Mom never said a word about Nancy listening in.

"Were you able to find this mystery person?" Mom asked.

"Not yet, but I'll be talking with every Erika in Tipton County if necessary."

"There has to be a more efficient way to do this." Nancy frowned. "Is there a factor you can use to rule out some of them?"

"Weight and height is all I have to go on."

Mom nodded. "That's something at least."

Nancy excused herself and added another serving of zucchini noodle lasagna to the oven to warm and pulled out the first portion she'd warmed. She'd made it from scratch, to ensure her mom wouldn't get anything unhealthy. After dividing the serving onto two small plates she called them to the table. "Lyle, give it ten minutes or so before you take out the rest."

"Why not nuke it?" He asked.

She placed her hands at her waist. "Because my mom doesn't need microwaved food in her body. Food cooked in an oven is healthier."

He raised his hands palms out. "Relax. It was only a question."

"I'm sorry. I didn't mean to overreact. I should go home now." She gave her mom a quick hug then left. She liked the change in Lyle. It was nice to finally have the man include her in a case without being coerced. Now to prove that his faith in her wasn't misguided. She needed to find this mystery woman who'd purchased the wig.

The following morning, Mary dressed in leggings and

a long-sleeved tunic top. Would she ever get warm? All her body wanted was sleep, but she needed to get a move on if she hoped to sneak in before Lyle or Carter saw her working. If either of them knew she was at work they'd have a fit—rightly so too. Fatigue dragged her down. Maybe she'd take a catnap then head over.

Mary awoke with a start. She'd seriously fallen asleep. What time was it? She stood and padded into the kitchen. The coffee pot had turned off since she'd had it set to turn on at four a.m. She enjoyed waking to the scent of freshly brewed coffee. Now the elixir was cold. How had she slept a whole hour when she'd only meant to sleep twenty minutes tops? That's what she got for pushing herself hard for so long—her body demanded she listen to it and give it the rest it needed. She poured a mug of coffee then heated it in the microwave. Unease she couldn't explain gripped her. On second thought, she'd make a fresh pot. What if someone had managed to get into her home while she slept and poisoned her coffee again?

Five minutes later she headed outside and nearly tripped over a foil covered box with a sticky note on top.

Thought you might enjoy a fresh slice of peach pie. Sincerely, Martha Jenson.

"Well, isn't that nice." Her neighbor had always been a kind woman. Mary squatted and picked it up, then raised the side of the foil and breathed in deeply of the scent of peaches. Her mouth watered. Though tempted to pull out a peach slice since there was no crust on top, she resisted. She placed the pie inside the door then locked up and turned to face her driveway. "Oh, stink." She stared at the empty driveway.

"You okay, Sheriff?"

Mary's gaze shifted to her neighbor who stood on the sidewalk in front of her home. "Good morning, Kent. It seems I'm without transportation until I go car shopping."

"Not a problem. I can take you wherever you need to go."

She studied her neighbor who rarely left his front porch. "You sure? I don't recall seeing you drive in recent years."

"I get out once a week. Today happens to be my get-out day. I can drop you off wherever you'd like and pick you up in a few hours. I meet some buddies down at Roaster's Coffee every Thursday morning. I was heading out when I spotted you." He motioned toward his car parked along the curb.

How had she missed seeing that? She shook her head. Maybe going to work was a bad idea, but now that she had a ride she didn't want to miss out on being there, even if it was only for a few hours. "I'd love a ride to the county courthouse."

"You got it." He turned and walked toward his old pickup.

Mary followed and slid onto the bench seat beside him and buckled in. "I appreciate the ride."

"It's my pleasure. It's not often I get to help someone." He signaled then pulled forward.

"This is going to come out wrong, but I'm curious about something." Mary glanced in her neighbor's direction. Maybe she should keep her mouth shut, but her need-to-know trait wouldn't let it go. "How is it that a man who spends hours a day sitting on his front porch is in such great physical shape?"

He laughed. "There are a lot of hours in a day. I enjoy gardening, and I've been a runner most of my life. I have gotten up with the sun for the past forty years. My home gym suffices for bad weather days."

"I had no idea."

He shrugged. "No reason you would. My Jackie loved to workout. It was her hobby, but she hated to go to a gym, and she didn't enjoy being outdoors."

"I'm sorry about your wife." The woman had died a couple of years ago. She went to sleep one night and never awakened. The coroner had said she'd died of natural causes. Kent had been stoic, but she imagined in private he'd had a lot to work through.

"Thanks. We were married late in life. Had celebrated our twentieth anniversary the week before she passed." He braked and pulled into the sheriff department's parking lot. "I'll meet you here at ten."

"Yes, sir. Thanks for the ride." She slid out and made her way inside. Fatigue slowed her steps—this had been a mistake, but there was no turning back now. She squared her shoulders and entered through the reception door. She breathed in the familiar scent of stale coffee and hard working bodies. It was good to be back. The bullpen beyond the reception desk grew silent. "Don't mind me." She strolled through the open space littered with desks and filing cabinets. "I'll be in my office, but I'm not here. Got it?"

Heads bobbed.

"Good." She closed the door then sank onto her desk chair. As feared, her to-do pile had doubled in size. Lyle had his hands full with the murder investigation. She imagined tackling her paperwork was the last thing he wanted to do. But she kind of liked it. There was something satisfying about seeing the stack of work shrink.

She slumped in the chair and rested her head back, closing her eyes.

"What are you doing here?"

Her eyes shot open. "Lyle."

"Mary." He closed the door behind him and stepped close to her desk with his arms crossed. "What are you doing here?" He repeated slowly.

Her pulse thrummed too fast. He'd called her Mary at work! She couldn't think of a time he'd ever done that. "You called me Mary."

"You called me Lyle."

He had her there. "But you never…"

"So?" He shot her a defiant glare.

"Why are you so angry?" Calling him by his given name shouldn't cause that.

"I stopped by your house, and when you didn't answer I broke in. I called the station to report you were missing, and I was told you were here."

"You broke into my house?" If she had the energy, she'd be angry. "What kind of damage did you do?"

"I picked the locks. You really need better locks."

She raised a brow. "For real?" It was bad enough a burglar broke into her home, but now Lyle? The moment she felt better she'd have a deadbolt that needed a key on the inside and out installed, and maybe an alarm system—no one else was getting into her home so easily. She should have had better security years ago, but Tipton had always been such a safe community she'd never felt the need.

"Yes. Now what are you doing here?"

"I have work to do."

"Nothing that won't keep. Besides that, I had planned to get to it soon."

"Now you won't have to." Assuming she could stay awake long enough to actually accomplish some work. "What time is it?"

"Seven thirty."

At least she only drifted off for twenty minutes. "My neighbor dropped me by. He'll return for me at ten."

Lyle narrowed his eyes. "Which neighbor?"

"Mr. Price. Kent. The man who—"

He waved off her reply. "I know who he is. He brought you over here, huh?"

"Yes. Guess he has a standing date with some buddies every week. By the way, I need a car. Want to go shopping with me this weekend?"

His mouth opened slightly before he snapped it shut. He studied her for a moment and his face softened. "You are supposed to be resting, not working or shopping for a car. How do you expect to return to work and win the election if you don't give your body time to heal?"

When he put it like that, she sounded rather immature and reckless. She shrugged.

"How about you look through what's on your desk, and I'll take you home in an hour?"

"That's not enough time." The stack would take half the day as sluggish as she was feeling.

He raised a brow.

"Fine. I'll stop in an hour." At least she'd make a dent in the stack. "I'll need to let Kent know I found another ride home."

"We can stop by Roaster's on our way to your place."

"How'd you know he's at Roaster's?"

"He's there every Thursday morning like clockwork. Although today he was a few minutes late."

"Are you telling me you were there too?"

"Pepper is an encyclopedia for local gossip."

Nancy's friend had the gift of gab and definitely had the pulse of their community. "Did you learn anything useful from her?"

"Maybe. Do you remember a woman named Wilma Wyatt?"

"The name's familiar. Give me some context."

"I dug into your old cases. You arrested her on a DUI about eight years ago."

"Okay, but what does that have to do with Pepper?"

"Pepper said she was back in town."

"Wonderful." Sarcasm dripped from her voice. The last thing they needed was a drunk putting their citizens in danger.

"It got me to thinking, so I looked at her case more thoroughly. She was a single mom. Her kids were put into the system when she was arrested."

"She couldn't have been in jail long."

"She wasn't," Lyle said. "But she lost custody for a while due to her addiction. Her record says she's a drug addict as well."

"Okay. I'm still not seeing the connection." She was too tired to be here if she couldn't follow what Lyle was trying to tell her.

"Maybe she has a vendetta against you."

Mary shook her head. "You really think she could be the one who killed Stan and then drugged me?"

"She has connections."

"Cyanide isn't exactly a street drug."

"Maybe not, but it puts her on my person-of-interest list."

"What about the wig lead?"

"I'm still working on it. But I was able to rule Lola out." Though that conversation still rang in his ears. That woman's filthy mouth would never need a microphone.

"Okay. I should wade through some of this before my time's up."

"What you should do is go home, but we both know that's not who you are." He sat in the chair across from her. "Hand me a stack. Maybe between the two of us, we can put a serious dent in this paperwork so you can rest easier."

She grinned. "I like this side of you."

"Don't get too used to it." A half smile lifted his cheek.

Chapter Ten

MARY WALKED INTO ROASTER'S AND IMMEDIATELY spotted Kent with his friends. Were they having a Bible study? Interesting. She figured they were here to shoot the breeze and gossip. She strode over to them with every ounce of energy she had left. "Excuse me, gentlemen."

Kent pushed his chair back and stood. "Did I lose track of time?"

"No. I wanted to tell you I have another ride home. Didn't want you to worry when I wasn't where we agreed to meet."

Kent glanced toward the window where Lyle sat in the cruiser waiting for her. "Thanks for letting me know. You have a pen and paper?"

She pulled them from her purse and handed it to him.

He wrote something on the top sheet then handed it to her along with the pen. "My number so you can call instead of tracking me down in the future."

She dropped it into her purse. "Thanks. I'll do that." She nodded to the other three men who silently watched their exchange. Without another word she left.

Lyle raised his chin toward the coffee shop as she eased onto the passenger seat. "How'd it go?"

"He gave me his number to call instead next time." She could have easily called Roaster's and they'd have given him a message, but her curiosity got the best of her. She wanted to know who his buddies were since she'd never noticed anyone visiting his home.

Lyle grunted as he pulled onto the road. "Mind if I stop by after my shift?"

"Not at all. What's up?"

He licked his lips. "I have an idea I want to run by you."

"Why not do it now? It'll take you five minutes to get to my place."

"It'll keep. Besides, I'm still mulling over the details in my head."

She nodded. "Want me to invite Nancy and Carter over too?" They'd always worked well together, but she couldn't stop the disappointment that it was work related. She'd sensed a shift in their relationship and thought he had as well, but considering what her body had been through, she could have imagined it.

"That's not necessary. You have any more of that lasagna Nancy made? I can't stop thinking about it— never expected lasagna to taste so good sans the pasta. Who would've thought thin strips of zucchini would make such a great substitute for the noodles."

"Sure do." She grinned. "I even have peach pie and vanilla ice cream for dessert."

"That's not exactly heart-healthy." He gripped the steering wheel so tightly his knuckles turned white.

"I'm a grown woman and can indulge once in a while if I so choose."

"Where'd you get the pie?"

"My neighbor, Martha. Jenson." The woman mostly kept to herself, so when she'd found it on her front porch it had been a pleasant surprise. "You know, she and Kent would make a nice couple. Maybe I should invite them over for a slice of pie since you're so against it."

"I'm not against pie per se, but don't you think it's a bit suspicious? After all, Stan died after eating pie."

She resisted rolling her eyes. "So I'm supposed to stop eating pie for the rest of my life? I'm sure the killer wouldn't use the same device twice." But just the same, the idea of a slice of pie no longer appealed.

"Probably not, but I'd think you'd be more cautious."

It was probably for the best. She could stand to lose a few pounds, and she was supposed to change her diet and exclude sweets. She sighed. "Kill joy." He didn't need to know she'd come to the same conclusion.

He eased to a stop in front of her house and put the car in park. "Please be careful, Mary. We don't know who to trust."

"I'm sure I can trust Martha. She's been my neighbor for years. If she wanted me dead, she's had plenty of opportunity to take me out." Though she spoke with confidence for Lyle's sake her gut told her that caution was prudent. Even if Martha wasn't out to get her, who's to say someone didn't spot the pie before she did and poisoned it? "Thanks for the ride." She got out. "See you later."

"Want me to come inside and make sure it's safe?"

"Do you really think that little of me?" Disappointment and indignation mingled.

"What are you talking about?" A blank look covered his face.

"I'm the sheriff. I think I can take care of myself."

"But you're still recovering."

"I'm a little tired." She shouldn't be so defensive, but fatigue had a way of bringing out her inner grouch. "I'll be okay. If it makes you feel better, I'll text in a minute after I've made sure everything is good inside."

"Or I could see for myself and save you the trouble."

"Relentless man." She grinned and closed the door. His concern was touching. She walked with a raised chin to the front porch and went inside. Her home looked exactly as she'd left it. She reached for her phone after making sure she was alone and shot off a text to Lyle.

All clear. Stop worrying. Thanks for caring.

Maybe she'd call and invite Martha over to join her for pie this afternoon. Even though she had no intention of eating it at this point, that would be the perfect way to determine if the woman had poisoned her or not. Martha wouldn't eat pie she'd sabotaged. She'd wrap up the case with one quick phone call, but she wouldn't hold her breath. She trusted Martha.

Lyle strode into the library. Maybe Nancy could talk some sense into her mother. Frustration seeped through every pore in his body. If he didn't know better, he'd say Mary had a death wish.

Nancy's face brightened when she spotted him

then she frowned and rushed to meet him a few feet from her desk. "What's wrong? Is my mom okay?"

"As far as I know she's fine, but you need to have a talk with her."

Nancy touched a finger to her lips and looked over her shoulder. "Let's go talk in the book mending room." She led the way down a short hall then unlocked a door to a room he'd never been in. She flicked on the light then leaned her hip against the counter. "What's going on?"

He explained about the pie and how reckless she was behaving. "She had no business going to work today. The doctor said she couldn't work for at least a week."

"I'll talk with her, but to be honest, if you couldn't get through to her, I don't think anything I say will either. Sometimes Mom is simply stubborn. This is probably her way of trying to maintain control."

He rubbed the back of his neck and sighed. He should have thought of that. Of course, Mary wanted—no needed—to be in control of her life. She was wired to take charge and be in command. With her surgery and the blasted election her life had been turned upside down.

"You okay, Lyle?" Consternation covered Nancy's face.

"I'm fine. I wanted to talk with your mom about something tonight, but now that I think about it, holding off would be best."

"You sure? Mom doesn't like to be kept in the dark about things."

A fact he well knew. But this was personal, not work related. "I'll think on it and decide later." Maybe

Nancy could help. He hated to admit to her what he'd been planning, but at the same time she might be able to offer advice. No. He didn't need advice. He'd stick to the plan, and if it fell flat then he'd take a long vacation to lick his wounds and retire at the end of the year. "Thanks for talking. You should probably get back out there." He motioned in the direction of the stacks.

"Laura's here, but you're right." She pushed off the counter and led the way. "I'll call my mom in a bit. I can't imagine she'd be so laissez-faire about the pie, even if it was from a trusted neighbor."

He squeezed her shoulder. "Thanks. See you around." He left and headed out. His cell rang. He checked the caller ID and his heart skipped. "Mary, what's up?"

"Thought you should know I invited my neighbor over for a slice of the pie she'd left on my front porch. You're never going to believe what she said."

"Don't keep me in suspense." He unlocked the cruiser and got behind the wheel.

"She didn't leave me a pie."

"I'm on my way." He threw the car into gear and pealed out. A few heads turned his direction. He radioed dispatch about the situation and that he was en route.

A few minutes later he parked along the curb at Mary's home. She stepped outside and raised a hand. "That was fast. Where were you?"

"The library." He hustled over to her.

She frowned. "Do I want to know?"

"Probably not." He didn't care to share why he'd gone to see her daughter. It would only make her angry. "Where's the pie?"

"Kitchen counter." She turned and headed inside. "For the record, I had no intention of eating it after our talk earlier, but I figured if she'd poisoned it, she'd decline coming over, and we'd have our killer. I didn't imagine she hadn't even left it."

He hadn't thought of that either but was grateful Mary hadn't lost her marbles like he'd feared. He took gloves from his pocket and slipped them on before picking up the pie. "I'll take this to the lab and have it tested."

"You think there will be prints?"

"I'm taking it in to test for poison, but I'll see if we can lift some prints. We know it will have yours for sure."

Her shoulders drooped and she looked down, avoiding eye contact. "Maybe I should pull out of the election and let Carter take over. Clearly, I'm not at the top of my game anymore."

"Mary, please look at me," he said gently.

She slowly raised her head until her uncertain gaze met his.

"No one expects you to be at the top of your game right now." Which was more than likely why the perpetrator had struck so soon after she returned home from the hospital. "You are supposed to be convalescing, not thinking about proper police procedure. No one expects anything from you except for you to rest and get well so you can return to work."

She nodded. "I know, but I feel so helpless here. I want to do something."

"Then give your body the rest it needs so you

can."

"I'll try." She looked so sad.

He didn't like seeing her like this. "Don't make dinner tonight. I'll take care of everything."

"But the food Nancy made needs to get eaten before it spoils."

"Freeze it." He placed a peck on her cheek without thinking. His face flamed. He turned and left without looking at her. What had come over him? He'd managed to go more than twenty years without a slipup. The stress of her life being threatened must have caused his blunder. He needed to pull it together. He had a murderer to find and distractions were dangerous.

Nancy knocked on her mom's front door after work before letting herself in. "Hey, Mom. It's only me." She closed and locked the door behind her then went in search of her mother. Mom wasn't on the couch, so she headed for the bedroom. "Mom?" She spoke softly in case she was asleep. Pushing the bedroom door open, she noted the empty bed. Where could she be? "Mom," Nancy called loudly as she two-timed it through the house.

The curtains leading to the patio were open. "That's odd." Mom almost never opened them. She headed to the door and looked outside. Her mother lay sleeping on a lounge chair. When did she get one of those? She slid open the door and stepped into the warm sunshine.

Mom's eyes fluttered open. "Nancy. What are you doing here?"

"Checking on you. I heard about the pie. I hope you didn't eat any of it."

Mom frowned. "Of course not. Lyle took it to the lab to have it tested for poison."

Nancy scrunched her face. "He did? What am I missing? I thought you planned to eat it? How did Lyle end up with it?"

Mom sat up and motioned her toward a chair. "Get comfortable." She updated her about the pie.

"Wow. Any word from the lab?"

"Not that I know. Can I ask you something?" Mom seemed hesitant.

Unease gripped Nancy. Mom was always confident. "Of course."

"When you saw Lyle earlier, did he seem off to you?"

"As a matter of fact, yes. He hasn't been himself since you were drugged."

"Okay. Thanks."

"That's it? Why did you ask?"

"Don't be nosy, Nancy."

"Nosy is practically my middle name," she said with a grin.

Mom chuckled. "You might have a point, but just the same."

Nancy blew out a breath and stood. "You should go inside. Your skin looks pink. How long have you been out here?"

"All afternoon."

"Mom. You know better than that." Nancy looked more closely at her mom's cheeks. They were much more than pink. At least she'd worn long sleeves and pants. "I'm surprised you didn't overheat with the way you're dressed."

"I've been cold ever since my surgery." She stood, and together they walked into the house.

Nancy looked around the house, noting it still looked spotless. "Want me to make you dinner?"

"No. Lyle is taking care of it tonight."

"He is?" Her voice raised a notch.

"Yes, and don't get any ideas. It's dinner, no big deal. We've had dinner here more times than I can remember."

"I know, but you always cook."

"I'm not up to cooking."

Nancy resisted rolling her eyes. Sometimes her mom could be so dense. She had a freezer full of food she only needed to reheat so there was no reason Lyle needed to bring dinner. "Is there something you're not telling me?" She teased.

"Nothing you need to know. Don't you and Anna usually walk together about now?"

Nancy glanced at the wall clock. "She'll wait."

Mom nudged her toward the door. "It's rude to be late. Thanks for stopping by. We can talk later."

"Sure thing, Mom. I want to hear all about your date with Lyle."

Mom practically pushed her out the door. "It's not a date."

"Mmm-hmm. Whatever you say." Nancy walked to her car with a spring in her step. Lyle was finally making a move—about time.

Chapter Eleven

LYLE RANG THE DOORBELL THEN WIPED his free hand down the side of his jeans as he stood outside Mary's front door. He was later than he'd planned to be.

The door opened and Mary stood there wearing a long sweater and leggings. She had to be roasting. Her hair fell in soft waves around her face—so much better than her usual ponytail.

"Rough day?" She stepped aside, allowing him to enter.

"No worse or better than normal. How about you?" Her flaming face gave him pause. "Looks like you got a bit of sun today."

"That's an understatement. Ever since my surgery I've been cold. I went outside to warm up and fell asleep. Thankfully, Nancy showed up when she did or who knows how bad of a burn I would have ended up with."

"That explains it." He walked to the kitchen and placed the takeout bag from Daisy's Diner onto the counter.

"Explains what?"

"The winter clothing in August."

She chuckled. "I suppose I do look a little odd." She eyed the bag. "What'd you bring us?"

"Roasted chicken, salad, and for dessert, berries."

"Anything from Daisy's will be delicious regardless of how healthy it sounds."

He grinned. She was on to him. He'd made it his personal mission to make sure she ate healthy. Not to disparage what Nancy had made for her mom, but some of the meals weren't as heart healthy as they should have been.

Mary pulled two plates from the kitchen cupboard while he unpacked the bag. He pulled back the foil that covered the chicken. "Mmm. That smells good."

"It really does." A soft smile lifted her face. "Any more progress on the case?" Hope filled her brown eyes.

"I have nothing new to report." He didn't want to talk about work or the case tonight. He needed a couple hours to give his brain a break. The lab results from the pie should be ready in the morning, but he suspected the pie had been laced with cyanide like the one that had killed Stan "It's too soon to know anything."

Her eyes dimmed. "Oh."

He reached out and grasped her hand. "Hey, you know how this works. It takes time to track down each lead."

She shrugged. "Somehow I'd hoped this case would be the exception and the murderer would confess or you'd catch a break."

He released her hand. "Not much chance of a confession. Now let's change the subject."

"Sure." She filled glasses with iced tea and brought them to the table.

He carried their plates to the table and set one in front of her. He sat and bowed his head then prayed a blessing over their meal. "Amen."

"Amen," Mary echoed. She eyed the food. "Daisy

makes delicious food."

He grinned. "You trying to talk yourself into eating it?"

"No. Not at all." She picked up her fork and knife and cut into the tender breast.

He stuffed his mouth with a large bite of chicken—as good as usual. The herb rub made all the difference. He motioned toward her plate. "Better eat up while it's still hot."

She took a bite of the chicken. Her brows rose. "This is really good."

"Of course it is. Daisy made it." He shook his head and made quick work of emptying his plate.

"Mind if I ask you a personal question?" Mary speared her salad.

"Not at all." Where was this going?

"You've been behaving out of character lately."

"That's not a question." He took a long drink of tea.

"I want to know why. You kissed my cheek earlier today and then tonight you held my hand. What's going on?"

He wiped his mouth slowly on a napkin. He'd planned to have this talk with her when he'd offered to bring dinner, then had changed his mind. He should have known she wouldn't let that kiss slide. "The thing is, I care about you. A lot. More than is prudent."

"Okay, but what changed between my heart attack and now?"

"I suppose I realized that we have no guarantee of tomorrow. Do you have any idea how hard it is to see someone you care about come close to death?"

"I wasn't going to die." She brushed at an imaginary crumb.

"You don't know that. If you hadn't already been in the hospital, you very well might have."

"But I didn't."

"For which I'm very thankful. The truth is, I've had feelings for you for a very long time. Your heart attack made me rethink my determination to keep things platonic between us. Life is too short." He dipped his chin. "I'm hoping you return my affection."

Mary blinked rapidly. "I never imagined having this kind of conversation. I thought my chance at love had expired, which is why I threw myself into my career and raising my daughter."

"It's not too late," he said softly. He reached for her hand. "What do you say?"

She shook her head. "I'm your superior. It's not appropriate."

"I'll quit."

"You can't quit," her voice raised an octave.

"Then what do you suggest?"

"I'll resign."

"No." He would not let her give up the career she loved.

She pushed back from the table and stood. "I'm a grown woman capable of making my own career decisions."

"And I'm a grown man capable of making mine."

His gaze locked with hers.

"Did you consider that maybe my heart attack made *me* re-evaluate my priorities?"

"I guess not. What conclusion did you come to?" He stood and tucked a hand into his jeans pocket.

"That I'm ready for a change."

"You kind of said much the same before. Have you figured out what that will look like?" He stepped closer to her. Could she be talking about them?

"I'm not sure yet." Her lashes lowered. "Contrary to what I said a moment ago, I don't think I should make any life-changing decisions while I'm recovering."

He blew out a breath. "You're right. I'm sorry. Forget I said anything."

She rested her hand on his shoulder. "Will you stop? I'm talking about my career, not you."

His heart beat wildly. "What about me?"

"I care more about you than any man I've ever known. You're my best friend and someone I know I can depend on. But I don't know how *we* could work when you are under my command."

"Can you see yourself loving me?" He swallowed the lump that had formed in his throat. He resisted the urge to fan his face. Did she have the heat on?

"I already do. But I'm not sure I should do anything about it. Yet." Her eyes pleaded with him to understand.

He raised his chin. "Okay." A man had his pride, and he would not beg or push her to figure this out tonight. He turned and cleared the dishes.

"You don't have to do that."

"I always help with the dishes." Plus he couldn't look at her right now. She loved him but was unwilling to do anything about it. Disappointment filled him. No. He needed to cut her some slack. She was right. This was not the time for her to be making life-altering decisions.

"Stop, Lyle." She held his arm still. "Please look at me."

He sighed. "Aw, Mary. Why are you doing this?" He finally met her gaze.

"Because I need my friend. Are we going to be okay?"

"Yes, but I should go home. It's been a long day."

Her eyes glistened. She stepped away from him. "Thanks for dinner. Will I see you tomorrow?"

He walked to the door. "I'll text the lab results. Stay safe." He walked out without looking back. Had he been a fool to tell her how he felt? At least she had the good sense to backpedal and not make a rash decision when she was still recovering.

His phone chimed indicating an incoming text message. He pulled out his cell. His jaw clenched. He turned and marched back to Mary's door.

Mary splashed water on her face. For the first time in days she was hot. Lyle had thrown her for a loop, but she should have seen it coming. It made total sense that after her brush with death he'd want to pursue his feelings. She wanted to also, but was it the right thing to do? *Lord I need your guidance. I love Lyle. We both want the same thing. But I don't know if it's wise. One of us would need to change jobs. Then again, I might not have a say in that.*

Her doorbell rang. She moved to the entryway and looked through the peephole. "Lyle?" She flipped the lock and yanked open the door. "What's wrong?" The expression on his face shot fear through her.

"Mind if I come in?"

She moved aside. "What's going on?"

"The lab results came back faster than expected. The pie tested positive for rat poison."

She balled her fists. "I feel so useless. I want to work this case, Lyle."

"No can do. Not until your doctor clears you."

"This is ridiculous. I realize I need to rest, and I can't run around following leads, but I can use my brain and investigating skills from here."

"You sound like Nancy."

"Well, she is my daughter." Now she knew how Nancy felt every time they'd told her to back off a case. Talk about frustrating. "I know you and Carter are great at what you do, but I *need* to help for my own sanity. Please, Lyle." She wasn't accustomed to begging, but life had done a 180 and things had changed.

He sighed. "Only if Nancy works with you."

Her mouth opened but no sound came out. She snapped it closed. This was so unlike Lyle.

"I can tell you don't like the idea."

"That's not it. I'm taken aback. Since when do you try and involve my daughter in one of our cases?"

"I've always had a soft spot for Nancy. You know as well as I do that she's already on the case. There's no way she'd sit this one out. She's too much like her mother." He winked.

Relief flowed through her. She'd been afraid things would be awkward between them now, but this was the Lyle she knew and loved. Yes, she really did love him, but it was an impossible love, wasn't it? Could they really follow their hearts and still be able to work together? What if what they thought they were feeling was simply heightened emotions because of everything that was going on? She needed to stop overthinking, but couldn't stop herself. She had a habit of analyzing things to death. Sadness consumed her.

He touched her arm. "Are you okay? Is it your heart?"

In a manner of speaking. She shook her head. "Ah. No. I'm okay."

He studied her face for a few seconds. "If you say so. I'll talk to Nancy and Carter about our plan. I'm hoping we can all meet up here tomorrow night."

That was too long to wait. "Can't you give me something to work on in the interim?" She would go stir crazy if she had to wait twenty-four hours to get started. She yawned. Then again, as tired as she was maybe she'd sleep all night and day then work all night tomorrow.

"I'll send you the photos witnesses took at the pie contest as well as a short video we acquired."

She blew out a breath. "Thank you." Finally, something tangible to do. "I thought we went through everything already."

"We did, but we must have missed something. I also need you to think about who benefits if you die."

No one but Nancy would benefit from her death. "You know Nancy is my sole heir. She'd never try to kill me."

"Think revenge. Or maybe someone wants you out of the picture because you're too good at your job. Were you working any covert cases? Could someone have found out?"

"I see where you're going." An idea niggled in the

back of her mind. It was a long shot. "I'll give this thought and hopefully have answers for you tomorrow."

"Good. You going to be okay here alone?"

She grinned. "I always am. Now shoo. My bed is calling." Mary nudged him toward the door and a moment later locked up. Still grinning, she headed to bed. She hadn't thought about it before now, but the DEA had reached out a few months back, regarding a suspected drug smuggling ring in Tipton County. She'd done some quiet snooping and discovered one of their drug mules. She'd told the DEA everything she'd discovered and left it at that. What if someone had learned of her involvement in the case and decided she was a threat? But wouldn't they have taken her out months ago? And why not shoot her? It would have been far quicker than poisoning a pie— this felt amateurish. Not like a professional hit.

Her phone rang. She checked the caller ID and didn't recognize the number. Should she answer? It was pretty late. Normally she would, but she was on medical leave so the call wouldn't be work related. She let it go to voicemail.

Her phone flashed that she had a new voicemail. She pressed the playback button.

"You've been lucky. Sooner or later your luck will run out. I know where you live," the digitally altered voice said. A shiver ran down her spine. How was she supposed to sleep after a message like that?

Chapter Twelve

Friday morning Nancy strolled into Roaster's Coffee and sat at her usual table. Her thoughts swam with all that had happened. Praise God, Mom was still alive. She had to figure out who was out to get her.

"Good morning." Pepper slid a plate with a chocolate donut in front of Nancy along with a cup of coffee, then sat across from her. "Sorry to keep you waiting. It's been busier than normal today."

"No problem. Any idea why it's so busy?" Nancy had noticed the buzz when she'd come in but hadn't thought much of it when her normal table sat vacant.

"Maybe." Pepper sipped from her mug. "I'm glad you made it. I wasn't sure you would with all that's been going on." She glanced toward the entrance.

"When have I ever missed this?" Pepper was acting odd. And what was up with *maybe* knowing what was going on? She opened her mouth to ask.

"Good point. So how are things?"

Nancy let her question go. There was no sense in grilling her. Pepper's secret-keeping skills were lacking. She'd tell her eventually if there was something to tell. "My mom is holding up well. Carter is super busy, and it feels like I hardly see him anymore, but that's to be expected, considering everything."

"I imagine it will only get worse if he wins the election."

Nancy nodded. "About that—do you have a feel for who the community supports?" She was caught in the middle of the two people she loved most in the world.

"Not really. Everyone feels awful about what happened to the sheriff. Believe it or not, I think someone trying to kill her actually helped her campaign."

"Crazy." Nancy bit into her donut and savored the chocolate flavor—perfection.

Pepper shrugged. "Did you hear about Stan's memorial service?"

"Yes. Today at one in the high school gym." A flier had been posted in several storefront windows about the memorial.

"Will you be there?"

"If I can slip away from work, but I'm not holding my breath. I've been depending on Laura way too much since my mom's accident and heart attack." She hadn't really known Stan, so her reason for going would be more to see who was there. She'd heard of killers showing up at their victim's funerals, but this technically wasn't a funeral so she wasn't sure.

A text chimed on Nancy's phone. She glanced at it and frowned.

"What's wrong?"

"It's Mom. She wants me to come to her house right now."

"That's odd. Did she say why?" An uneasy expression rested on Pepper's face.

"No." Nancy narrowed her eyes. "What aren't you telling me?"

Pepper wrapped Nancy's donut in a napkin and

thrust it toward her then

reached for her coffee. "I'll get you a to-go cup."

"Pepper, what do you know?" Nancy followed her to the counter.

"There are some reporters in town. They were asking about Stan's murder and funeral and then started talking about the election." Pepper poured the remainder of her coffee into a to-go cup, topped it off, then popped on a lid and handed it to Nancy.

"Did you tell them where my mom lives?" Nancy couldn't believe her friend would do that, but why else would she be behaving so odd?

"Of course not. But they're reporters. They know how to figure out that kind of stuff."

"Good point. I better get over there." Nancy raised the coffee cup to her lips. She needed every drop of caffeine she could get. "Thanks for this."

Pepper sucked in her bottom lip.

Compassion filled Nancy. Her friend probably blamed herself, and they didn't even know if there was a reporter bothering her mother. "Hey, everything will be okay. Mom knows how to take care of herself. Don't worry."

"I know. But it's hard not to worry, considering all that has been going on in this town and with you and your family."

"Tell me about it, but I have faith everything will be okay." She had to have faith, otherwise she'd go crazy with worry.

Pepper squared her shoulders and raised her chin. "Me too. But let me know when you get there that your mom is okay."

"I will. 'Bye." Nancy strode out and headed for her

Mustang. She pressed her mother's name in the contact list on her phone and put it on speaker as she got in.

Mom answered after two rings.

"Are you okay?" She winced at the panic in her voice.

"Yes. But I need a ride."

"To where?" Nancy pulled out and headed in the direction of her mom's place.

"The courthouse."

"You're on medical leave." Why hadn't Mom mentioned any reporters?

"I know, but this is important and there's no better place for me right now."

Nancy sighed. "Why? You won't get the rest you need there."

"I received a phone call last night that makes me think not being at home would be best for my well being."

Uh-oh. "Tell me about it?" This sounded way worse than a reporter asking a few questions.

"I'll play it for you when you get here."

Nancy pulled into the driveway. "I'm outside."

"I'll be right out." Mom exited, carrying a large duffel bag.

Nancy sprung from the car. "You aren't supposed to lift more than five pounds." She jogged to the porch and took the strap off her mom's shoulder.

"Thanks. I didn't think it was a big deal. It's not too heavy."

She was right, but it had to weigh at least ten pounds, well over the limit. "What's in here?" Nancy asked as she walked to the passenger side of the car then pulled open the door.

"A blanket, pillow, toiletries, and a few changes of clothes."

Nancy hesitated, leaving her hand on the door. "Why?"

"It's not safe here."

"Okay." That was all Nancy needed to hear. Her practical, no-nonsense mother would only do something like this if necessary. Nancy closed the door then hustled to the driver's side and got in. "What happened?" She backed out then headed for the courthouse.

"I'll play the message." Mom pulled out her phone and held it toward Nancy.

Nancy listened. Her pulse thrummed in her ears. She wasn't accustomed to fearing for her mother. "This kind of thing doesn't happen to you all the time? I assume you've made plenty of people angry through the years."

"That's true, but no one has ever called my private number."

Now Nancy understood. Mom didn't give that number out to just anyone. It was reserved for those who absolutely needed it. "Maybe someone with your number in their contact list had their phone stolen. It might not be someone you know."

"I've considered that."

"But you don't think that's the case."

"That's what I aim to find out. Besides you, everyone who has my private number also works at the courthouse."

"So you're not going there to stay safe?" Sometimes Mom could be so confusing.

"Nope. But I want everyone there to think that's why I'm there. Should the perpetrator be in that building, I want him to think he's gotten to me."

"I thought it was a woman, based on the video surveillance."

"In this case I'm using he as a gender-neutral word."

"Okay. So we're on the same page, I'll do the same." Nancy pulled into the Sheriff Department's parking lot and killed the engine. "How will you figure out who is behind all of this, assuming they are here?"

"Doing what I do best. Talking to people and reading their body language. I'll know. I only need to ask the right question to the right person."

"Hmm. Okay. Before you go in, there's something you should know."

Mom sighed. "Why do I get the feeling this isn't good news?"

"Depends on how you look at it." Nancy tried to make her voice chipper. "Pepper said a couple of reporters were in town asking about you, the election, and Stan. I thought maybe they were the reason you called me."

"Thanks for the heads up, but so far I haven't been approached."

Nancy motioned toward the courthouse. "They're probably inside."

"You could be right." Mom opened the car door.

"I'll carry your bag in then I need to get to the library." She'd barely get there in time, but she wouldn't leave Mom to fend for herself. She got out, grabbed the duffel, and accompanied her mother inside. They walked into the bullpen and the hum of activity hushed.

"Don't mind me," Mom said. "I'm not here." Without waiting for a response Mom marched to her office.

Nancy closed the door behind them. "Are you sure about this?"

"I thought about it all night and this was the best idea I came up with. Did you notice any reporters lurking about?"

"Nope. I wonder where they went." If she wasn't in such a hurry to open the library, she'd figure it out, but as it stood, Mom would have to deal with this on her own. She'd shoot Lyle and Carter a text to make sure they knew what was going on. "I'd better head out. If you need anything, let me know."

"How about dinner?"

Nancy grinned. "I'll swing by and pick you up on my way home from work. You can eat with us tonight."

"That'll work. Hopefully by then I'll have a suspect."

"Be careful, Mom."

"Always."

"And don't overdo. I still need you." Her voice caught and she cleared her throat.

Mom blinked rapidly. "You better get a move on."

"Right." Nancy left, wishing more than anything she could stick by her mother's side. She had to trust her husband and Lyle would make sure she was okay. Mom needed an ally she could trust implicitly— Lyle was that man.

Mary closed her office door and blinds. What she needed to do required the utmost secrecy. She pulled the secure phone from a locked drawer in her desk and placed the call she'd been putting off.

"Agent Davis." The DEA agent in charge of the operation she'd assisted in sounded exactly like she remembered—impatient and in charge.

"This is Sheriff Daley from Tipton County. I have a problem." She explained what had been going on. "I'd like to read-in a small team of people I trust."

"I don't think this case is related, but on the off chance it is, I'll cooperate. We appreciated your help and hope to be able to count on you in the future."

"Thank you, sir."

"I'll need names, and they will have to be cleared before you give them the basics. Only what they must know. Understood?"

"I understand." She gave him the list of names. "Do you need anything else?"

"Not at this time. Are you certain this is absolutely necessary? Like I said, we want to use you again and this might make it difficult to do so if word gets out."

"I wouldn't ask if I didn't trust each of them implicitly. Please put a rush on clearing my people."

"I'll do my best."

"Thank you." She slid the phone into her pocket, praying it wouldn't take long. The sooner she could read her team in on this the quicker they could confirm or eliminate a connection.

Now to pay her respects to Stan. She stood and

headed out. Kent waited along the curb nearby. She opened the door and got in. "I appreciate the ride."

"I'm happy to help. Will you want a ride back to the courthouse after?" He pulled away from the curb.

"I'll call if so. I might be able to hitch one from someone at the service."

"Okay. How's your investigation going? Are you any closer to solving the murder?"

"Every time we rule out a person of interest, I believe we get a little closer to the perpetrator."

"Way to keep a positive attitude." He pulled into Tipton High School's parking lot and drove toward the gymnasium. "There's a good turnout. Glad I don't have to park. Not sure there's an empty spot anywhere. I'll drop you off as close as possible."

"I appreciate that."

He pulled to a stop along the curb several feet from the entrance. "Here you go."

"Thanks. I owe you."

"Now, don't you try and repay me. That takes all the joy out of me being neighborly."

She paused with her hand on the door and gave him a smile. "Okay. Thanks." She got out and strolled inside. The high school gymnasium would more than likely be packed with former students and their parents, along with staff and community members.

She found an end seat on the bleachers near an exit. A camera crew from a Portland news station had set up a spot to interview guests. She blew out a breath. She'd do her best to avoid the reporter and camera.

It looked like half the town had turned out to remember Stan. Clearly many people cared about the man whose life was cut short. He must have made a strong impact on the lives he touched.

Principal Gains held a microphone to his mouth, but Mary had no idea what he said. Her attention focused on observing all of those in attendance. The chance that the killer was here was good. She pulled out her phone and casually filmed those in the stands. She would never be able to remember everyone here.

After several people spoke about Stan, two high school students sang "Amazing Grace" to close the service. As they finished the hymn, Mary stood, anxious to escape the gymnasium before the press spotted her.

She slipped out the nearest exit then positioned herself in an out-of-the-way corner.

"I figured I'd find you here."

She whipped her head in the direction of Lyle's voice. "What are you doing here?"

"Same as you, I imagine."

"You stick out like a red cherry on an ice cream sundae in your uniform."

His eyes twinkled as he licked his lips. "I like that imagery."

She chuckled. "I got this. Unless you need something, scram."

He grinned. "You're feisty. You must be feeling better. I'll wait outside in my cruiser. When you're ready to head back, text me."

She nodded. As much as she enjoyed his company, she needed to blend in to be able to observe the people in "the wild." If no one noticed her, they would more than likely be themselves.

The main doors to the gymnasium opened and the crowd surged out. A few minutes later Mayor Charlie and his daughter exited with linked arms. May's eyes were swollen and red. Several high school students with red-rimmed eyes followed.

This town needed something positive to focus on. The end of summer was supposed to be a fun time, not a time of mourning.

After a while, no one else left the gym, so she shot off a text to Lyle and headed outside. The reporters hadn't given her a second look when they'd followed the crowd. Her plan to blend in seemed to have worked. Being out of uniform had been the right decision.

Now to get back to her office and process all she had seen and heard.

Lyle sat beside Mary at Nancy's table. Carter and his nephew were across from them.

Nancy carried a platter with a roast on it to the table. "I'm so glad I put this in the crockpot this morning."

"It smells delicious," Lyle said.

"Yeah." Carter stood to clear a space for the large platter. "My stomach has been rumbling since I walked in the door."

"Well, the wait is over." Nancy sat to Carter's right.

After Carter blessed the food, they dug in.

Nancy looked Lyle's way. "I assume Mom told you about the phone call."

He nodded. How much could they say in front of

Gavin? He was a good kid, but the more people who knew what was going on, the greater the risk.

Mary speared a slice of meat. "We can talk about this later."

It sounded as though he and Mary were on the same page—good. At least he knew she wanted him to stay quiet.

"A reporter and camera guy were at the high school today for the memorial service." Gavin forked a bite of roast into his mouth.

"Did you talk to them?" Lyle looked at Gavin then exchanged a glance with Carter. Nancy had alerted them to the press being in town. He had done a little digging and learned a news station had sent a crew down to cover the murder and election. It was interesting that they'd crashed the memorial service.

"No."

Carter pushed the food around on his plate. "Why not? They didn't seek you out? For some reason I thought they'd want a quote about the election from you."

"I was with Mr. Gains when they stopped me." Gavin shrugged. "He told them I was a minor, and they couldn't talk to me without your permission."

Carter grinned. "Guess it pays for me to be friends with your principal."

Gavin grunted.

Lyle chuckled. He'd heard they had interviewed Mayor Wallace, but Mary had managed to dodge the woman and her cameraman. Too bad they hadn't called ahead. At the very least Carter could have given them a sound bite, but as it stood, he'd been out of town all day working a lead that had turned out to be nothing.

Gavin wiped his face with a napkin. "May I please be excused?"

"That was fast," Carter said.

"I have a date. Remember?"

Carter's eyes twinkled. "I didn't forget. Have fun bowling."

"We will. Thanks." Five minutes later they heard the front door close a little too hard.

Nancy blew out a breath. "I didn't think he'd ever leave."

They all laughed.

Lyle cleared his throat. "I think talking to the media is a good idea."

Everyone's attention shifted to him.

"It's a good human-interest story." Lyle could tell he'd shocked his friends. "And you never know, the perpetrator might make a wrong move if they panic due to the media's interest."

Mary appeared to be considering his idea. "I suppose if he likes the attention it could draw him out."

"Exactly," Lyle said. Mary was a smart woman. It had only taken her a second to see where he'd been going with his suggestion. "Are you onboard, Carter?"

Carter stuffed a big bite of meat into his mouth and chewed slowly.

Nancy playfully slugged him. "That's his way of stalling for time."

Lyle knew so he only nodded.

Carter reached for his glass of water and took a long draw then set it down. "In theory your plan is sound, but it could backfire. He might intensify his tactics. He wants the sheriff dead."

"This has gone on long enough, Carter," Mary said. "We aren't at work. It's okay to call me Mary or Mom."

Carter shook his head. "Can't."

"You could win the election." Mary raised a brow. "Then what will you call me?"

"Guess I'll have to figure that out if it happens. Now, back to finding this guy."

Nancy huffed out a breath. "Or gal."

"That goes without saying, hon." Carter draped an arm across the top of the chair in which Nancy sat. "I have a theory."

"What's that?" All three asked in unison.

"I've been through all of your old cases. I investigated anyone who had motive to kill you, and they all have alibis including Wilma Smith, who was our most promising lead from your old cases. I'm beginning to think this attack is personal." Carter looked at Mary.

Mary sighed. "There is one other possibility not in our records. I contacted the DEA today to get permission to share this with all of you."

Lyle frowned. What was Mary talking about?

"I worked on a joint task force operation recently with the state police and DEA. I made a key arrest, and the DEA processed him."

Nancy's face paled. "Are you saying drug cartels could be after you?"

Mary shook her head. "I seriously doubt that. Poisoning pie isn't their style."

"Then what *are* you saying?" Lyle couldn't believe she'd kept this to herself. Then again, she was the boss and didn't need to report to him.

Mary ran her finger along the rim of her glass. "Only that there is a possibility this could be related to drugs. The cartel wouldn't waste their time with poison, but maybe a loved one of the man I put away would."

"How would they know you had anything to do with his arrest?"

"He easily could have told them."

Lyle pulled out his notepad and pen. "Do they live in Tipton County?"

"As a matter of fact, yes." She went on to tell them about the man's family who lived at the edge of the county line.

Lyle couldn't wait to wrap up this case. The sooner they arrested the murderer the better. "Sounds like Carter and I need to pay the family a visit."

Nancy tilted her head to the side. "Why didn't you say anything about this sooner, Mom?"

"Everything happened so fast, then I had my heart attack. I didn't think of him at first, and then it took time to get cleared to let you know about the operation."

It made sense. Especially with Nancy being a civilian. "Want to head out there tonight, Carter?"

The man shook his head.

"Why not?" How could Carter say no?

"We can go there at first light. I want to be able to see what we are walking into. They aren't expecting us, and it will give us time to plan."

Lyle's face heated. He knew better. His rush to act could've gotten them both killed if he'd acted on his impulse. At least one of them was thinking clearly.

Chapter Thirteen

NANCY STARED AT THE PAGES OF a mystery she'd
ordered for the library as she sat on a lounge chair in
her backyard. Mom rested beside her. How could she
sleep when Lyle and Carter were confronting the
family of the person she'd put away? Wasn't she
worried or anxious? Nancy sure was. What if
something went wrong? Or what if they weren't
behind the attacks on Mom? They were out of leads.

Mom tilted her head toward her. "Will you please
relax?"

"I am relaxed."

"Yeah, right," Mom said. "And I'm twenty-five and
the picture of good health. You haven't turned a
single page for the past twenty minutes."

Nancy sighed. "You're too observant for my good."

Mom chuckled. "Observation is in my DNA."

Nancy rolled her eyes. "How can you be so
relaxed?"

"I trust Lyle and Carter. They are very good at
their jobs. But more importantly, my faith is in the
Lord."

Would she ever learn to have the kind of faith her
mother had? She wanted it, but it didn't come as
naturally as it seemed to for Mom. "So you're not
worried in the slightest?" She held her thumb and
index finger slightly apart.

"Worried no. Anxious? Maybe a bit. I'd like for

this to be over, so I can go about my daily activities without putting anyone else in harm's way."

That sounded exactly like her mom. Always worried about the people around her. Which made complete sense, considering the profession she'd chosen.

Mom's phone vibrated. She picked it up and read the screen. She sighed, rested her head back and closed her eyes.

"Was it the relatives?"

"No."

"Now what?"

"We keep digging. Sooner or later this person is going to make a mistake, and when he does, we'll be ready."

Nancy shifted in her seat and faced her mom. "What if it's someone we all know? Someone in our day-to-day lives?"

"It wouldn't be the first time a criminal was among us. We need to stay vigilant." Mom's jaw jutted.

"I know, but how long can we reasonably stay vigilant? No one can be on alert all the time for an extended period. It's too much." And if it was someone in their day-to-day life, sooner or later they could succeed in their goal to kill her mom. She couldn't allow that to happen.

"Then you better put your sleuthing skills to use."

Nancy's eyes widened. "Are you giving me your blessing to work on this?"

"In the beginning, I wanted to keep you as far away from me and this case as possible, but I don't see how I have any choice now. Besides, Lyle has kept you up to date. It's not like he made a secret of it." She reached for her glass of ice water on the ground beside her and took a sip. "You look at the world through a different lens than people in law enforcement do, and it works. So go for it, but be careful. I'd never forgive myself if something happened to you because I read you in on this case and gave you my blessing to follow your instinct."

Nancy stood. "I will. I promise. I'm going inside. Will you be okay on your own for a while?"

"Of course. What are you going to do?"

"I want to review the pictures we have from the day of the pie contest."

"I can't imagine what you'll find." Doubt covered Mom's face. "I've studied them ad nauseam and couldn't find anything useful."

"Weren't you the one who said I look at things differently?"

"Point taken. Go. I'll be fine."

Nancy rose and gave her mom's shoulder a gentle squeeze. "I'm only a holler away if you need anything."

Mom patted her hand.

Two hours later, Nancy still hunched over her kitchen counter with photographs spread out everywhere. She'd printed all the pictures. Call her old fashioned, but there was something about being able to hold a copy of a photograph in her hand that helped her think more clearly.

She wrote out the name of every person she knew in the pictures. Maybe Anna could identify the rest. She shot off a text to her neighbor, and five minutes later a knock sounded on Nancy's door. She pulled it open and grinned. "You're quick."

Anna breezed in. "This is way more exciting than doing laundry."

Nancy motioned toward the kitchen. "I have all the photos on the counter. How about you go through each one, listing the names of everyone you recognize, and I'll write them down?"

"Sounds good to me." Anna studied the photos and thirty minutes later they'd identified almost everyone. She rubbed her lower back. "There were a lot of people there. Is everyone on the list a suspect?"

"Not officially, but to my way of thinking they are. Anyone in the tent had access to the pies."

"Right, but you said that the mayor was instructed to give the first round to your mom."

"True, but he has no idea who sent the email, and we couldn't track it."

Anna frowned. "Seriously?"

"Well, they checked the IP but it didn't help. It's all very technical and my mind shut off when it was being explained. All that really matters is that they couldn't find the person."

"Got it. You know whomever did this took a huge risk. It only takes a drop of Cyanide on your skin to kill you. Either this person was well covered, or too stupid to know the seriousness of the poison."

"Maybe the risk was worth it."

"But why? What did your mom do to motivate that kind of hate?"

"I can't begin to understand the mind of a murderer, but I do know that unforgiveness left to fester can easily turn to hate. Maybe mom slighted someone without knowing."

"That's some serious hate." Anna's brow creased. "I once had a student hate me because I kept her after class for a couple of minutes. Apparently, it embarrassed her when I asked in front of the entire class for her to hold up because I needed to discuss something with her."

"How'd you find out? Did she do something to you?"

"No. But her attitude changed. I ended up requesting a conference with her and her parents. That's when she finally told me what I had done and why she hated me."

"Wow. What did you do? Is she still in high school?"

"She graduated a few years ago. I apologized and have done my best to not embarrass my students since then. It's certainly a challenge, but I try to learn from things like that."

"So what you're saying is that even a perceived slight could cause a person to snap."

Anna shrugged. "I guess so."

"If that's the case, anyone in this town could be suspect." Nancy studied the list of people in the pictures. Pepper's name was among her list of suspects. But there was no way she'd try to kill Mom. Plus, Pepper wasn't one to hold a grudge. Besides, Carter had already cleared her friend. Nancy crossed her name out.

"How are you sure it wasn't Pepper?"

"Besides the fact that Carter already spoke with her, my gut. If she was going to kill anyone, it would have been me." She chuckled. "When I was planning, or rather, not planning my wedding, I think she wanted to wring my neck, yet she never did. She's innocent."

Anna grinned. "Now you kind of sound like a cop."

Nancy grinned. "Thanks." She admired those in law enforcement. "But I don't want to think like one. Mom said my ability to see things differently than a cop is what makes me valuable in this situation."

"That was nice of her."

The wistful tone in Anna's voice gave Nancy pause. She studied her friend and frowned. "Why are you home alone on a Saturday? Don't you, Luke, and Maddie usually do something?"

"Yes, but Maddie is out of sorts, so Luke thought he should spend some alone time with her."

"Good for him. That's a switch from what he used to be like. You've been a great influence on that man."

"Thanks, but I wish he would have included me. I feel like I could have gotten through to Maddie."

"You probably could have, but he's her dad, he should get first dibs."

Anna chuckled. "You have a funny way of putting things, but I do see your point."

"FYI, I suspect she's feeling left out. Gavin and Maddie's friend, Ciara, went on a date. With school starting soon, Maddie probably feels anxious about not having anyone to hang out with at lunch if Gavin and Ciara become an item."

"Maybe, but surely they'd include her too." Confusion covered Anna's face.

"I would hope so." Nancy frowned. "I warned Gavin this could happen. I imagine Maddie feels like she lost her two best friends and regrets setting them up."

"I don't know. It can't be that serious. Haven't they only gone on one date?"

Nancy nodded. "But they spent all morning together today at the skateboard park."

"She's a skateboarder?" Anna's voice held surprise. "I thought she was more the studious type."

"One can be studious and enjoy riding a skateboard." Nancy moved to the fridge. "Would you like anything to drink?"

"Water, or iced tea if you have any."

Nancy had made sun tea yesterday so she pulled the jar from the fridge and poured a glass for each of them. She took them to the table and sat.

Anna joined her. A worried look rested on her face.

"Are you thinking about Maddie or my mom?"

"Maddie. I want to help her, but I don't know how." Anna had a soft spot for the teen and had been going out of her way to help the girl long before she started dating Luke. Her face brightened. "What if I try and set her up with a boy? Do you think she'd like that?" She shot Nancy a hopeful look.

"No way. I realize you're the resident expert when it comes to teens, but I think staying out of it is the best thing you can do for now."

Anna's shoulders rolled forward slightly. "I suppose." She tipped her head to the side. "Maybe she'd enjoy a girls' day at the spa."

"Maddie?" Nancy shook her head. "You do know who we're talking about, right?"

"Just because she doesn't spend hours on her makeup, hair, and clothes doesn't mean she wouldn't enjoy a manicure or a new haircut."

"I suppose." Nancy sipped her tea. The answer behind Stan's murder had to be in those pictures. She stood and walked back to the counter. She pointed to a mousy looking woman standing beside the table. Her gaze was turned away from the camera. What was she looking at?

"Anna, come look at this."

Her friend moved to her side. "What am I looking at?"

Nancy pointed to the blonde woman. "See how she's looking off to the side? What do you think she sees? Or is she up to no good and trying to determine if she's being watched?"

"It sort of looks like she's thinking to me. I sometimes hold my eyes like that when I'm pondering something."

Nancy bit down on her bottom lip. "Hmm. Maybe. But I don't know. We need to find out who this woman is and if she had a pie entered into the contest."

"Charlie ought to know. He seems to be acquainted with everyone in this town."

"Great idea. I wonder how he'd feel about me stopping over at his house on a Saturday?"

A gleam lit Anna's eyes. "Let's find out." She turned and headed for the door. "Wait. My mom is out back. I can't leave her here alone."

Anna frowned. "I suppose she could come too."

"Maybe. Be right back." She strode to door and poked her head outside. "Mom, Anna and I are taking a drive. Want to come along?"

Mom waved her off. "The men are on their way

and will be here any minute. I'll be fine."

Nancy hesitated. "Are you sure?"

"Yes. I know how to take care of myself."

Nancy closed the door, then confirmed with Carter he was close to home. She grabbed her keys and purse and followed after Anna. "Carter is right around the corner, so she'll be fine." She locked up then hustled to her car and slid inside.

Anna eased beside her. She whistled softly. "I think this Mustang might be even nicer than your wrecked one."

"Thanks. I've been working at restoring this baby ever since Carter surprised me with her." Nancy turned the key and the engine purred to life. "What if Charlie isn't home?"

"It's a small town. We'll find him."

Nancy chuckled as she backed out of her driveway. "I don't know what's come over you, but I like your sense of adventure."

Anna grinned. "Bring it on."

Nancy laughed. "Better watch what you say. You might get more than you bargained for."

"Don't I know it." She sobered.

Anna had had more than her share of adventure. Thankfully, her life had calmed down and settled into an easy rhythm. Which might be the very reason her friend was eager to help now. Once a person had a taste of adventure it was difficult to go without for long.

Nancy eased to a stop in front of Charlie's home. A tingle shot through her. Were they doing the right thing? Would Carter and Lyle have a fit? She shook off her apprehension and stepped out of her car, joining Anna on the sidewalk.

"Are you okay?" Anna asked.

"A little nervous, but I'll be fine."

"Why are you nervous?" Anna's brow furrowed.

"I don't know." It wasn't like her to get nervous like this. Especially when talking to their mayor. He wasn't an intimidating person. She squared her shoulders and marched toward the front door.

Anna rang the bell.

A moment later May opened the door. "Nancy. Anna. This is a surprise." She opened the door wide. "Come in out of the heat."

"Thank you." Nancy stepped inside. Cool air washed over her. The house smelled fresh and clean. Nancy smiled. "Anna and I were hoping to talk with your dad. Is he home?"

"He's out back. It's so rare for us to have guests pop in. Do you have time to sit for a visit?"

Nancy held in a sigh. She didn't want to visit with May but she couldn't be rude. "Of course. How have you been?"

May's face fell. "Horrible. With Stan's murder and a killer on the loose, I can hardly sleep at night. On the bright side, the house has never been cleaner. Since I can't sleep, I clean." She guided them through the palatial home to a sunroom in back. A cross breeze cooled the space. "Please have a seat, and I'll grab us a pitcher of cucumber water." She rushed from the room.

Anna sat and wrinkled her nose. "Cucumber water? It sounds fancy."

Nancy joined her on the off-white settee. "Not really. It's sliced cucumber in water. It flavors the water. I've seen it done with strawberries too."

"Sounds perfectly disgusting."

"Shh. She's coming."

May set a tray holding three tall glasses of ice water onto a coffee table and sat in the rocker. "How is your mom doing, Nancy?"

"Oh, you know her. Nothing keeps her down for long."

May nodded and reached for a glass. She sipped it. "I'm not much of a water drinker, but when it's flavored it's not bad." She focused on Anna. "How is the school handling the loss of Stan? I'm sure he will be hard to replace. He was an amazing man."

Anna shifted. "They're working on finding a replacement. He will be missed."

Amazing man? "Did you know Stan well, May?" Nancy asked.

"Oh, yes. We'd actually dated some this summer." Sadness filled her eyes. "I still can't believe he's gone. I sure hope the police find who is responsible soon."

"We do too," Nancy said. "I see your dad is taking a break in the shade. Would now be a good time to talk with him?"

"I suppose." She stood and opened the screen door. "Daddy, you have guests." She motioned at Nancy and Anna to head out.

Nancy spoke to Anna out the side of her mouth. "Let me do the talking."

"No problem."

Charlie stood. "Ladies, what brings you by?"

Nancy pulled the photo from her purse. "We were wondering if you know who this woman is?"

He gave the photo a quick look. "I believe her

name is Sara. She's quiet and keeps to herself for the most part. I'm surprised she was at the pie baking contest."

"Did she enter?" Nancy asked.

"As a matter of fact, yes. Do you think she could be the murderer?"

"That's not for us to say." Nancy did not want him to know she was investigating the case. "I was showing Anna the pictures I had from that day and neither of us knew who she was. It was driving us both crazy. We figured you'd know."

His chest puffed out. "I try to make a point to meet all my constituents." He rubbed his chin. "She's certainly close enough to the table to have slipped poison into the pies."

"Now, Charlie," Anna said. "That's how rumors are started and lives are ruined."

He bobbed his head. "Thank you for pointing that out. I wouldn't want to sully the reputation of an innocent person."

"What more can you tell us about Sara?"

"Not all that much. She and her husband moved to town about four months ago. They don't have any children. He works for the Parks and Rec department."

"What does she do?" Nancy asked.

"She works from home, crafting. She sells her work online from what I understand."

"I didn't realize a person could make a living that way." Anna sounded impressed.

"One can try." Charlie brushed a patch of dust from his cargo shorts. "Is there anything else I can help either of you with?"

"Nope." Nancy grinned. "Your yard is looking nice."

"Thanks. It's a labor of love."

Nancy smiled. "We should go and let you get back to your hedges." She motioned toward the photinias along the back fence and walked toward the gate.

"What are you doing?" Anna asked softly.

"Making a run for it. If May corners us inside again, we'll never get out of here." She opened the gate and they made a smooth escape. Nancy breathed a little easier.

"I kind of feel sorry for her," Anna said.

Nancy glanced at her friend. "Why?"

"She still lives with her dad for starters. And she lost a man she clearly cared about. I don't know what I would do if something happened to Luke."

"I imagine you're right about her hurting. Which is probably why she can't sleep. That's got to be rough." Nancy felt for the woman. "However, you are strong. You'd go on living and being a productive member of society."

"I know, but my heart would be shattered into a million tiny pieces."

Nancy nodded, knowing she'd feel the same way should any harm come to Carter. She loved him more than she ever imagined possible. She got behind the wheel and started the engine.

Anna buckled in beside her. "Where to now?"

"My place. We'll do a little digging into Sara and see what we can find out about her. See if she has a reason to want my mom dead and check her alibi for the evening Mom's home was broken into."

"I thought a man broke into her place."

Nancy shrugged. "It could have easily been a woman. No one saw the person's face and their build was non-descript."

"Okay. Shouldn't the police question her?"

Nancy eased off the gas. "Good point. I'll let Carter and Lyle know what we found out." Then she'd do some digging online and see what she could learn about the woman.

Chapter Fourteen

Sunday afternoon Mary watched from the two-way mirror as Lyle questioned Sara McGovern, a thirty-year-old entrepreneur. Normally they wouldn't have used the interrogation room, but Mary wanted to watch the interview without Sara knowing she was listening in. How did someone who looked so timid and understated make a success at business? Clearly looks were deceiving, particularly where Mrs. McGovern was concerned. Mary could hear everything they said in the room, but so far Lyle had kept the conversation light.

Lyle slid a photograph across the table. "I requested you come here today to ask you about the day Stan Gibson died. Did you know him?"

Mary observed the woman's expression and body language closely. Her eyes widened ever so slightly at the question, but she showed no sign of distress.

"I knew he was running for sheriff. That's the extent of my knowledge about him."

Lyle wrote on his notebook then looked back at Sara. "Why did you try and remove the tray of pies from the judges table?"

Sara's face paled. "I had no idea they were poisoned. I had nothing to do with that."

Either the woman was quick thinking or guilty since she had followed Lyle's trail without having it spelled out to her. Mary hadn't yet decided.

"Are you acquainted with Sheriff Daley?"

She shook her head. "We'd never met until that day when she ordered me to leave the pies alone. I was only trying to help. I thought having the area cleared around that poor man would be helpful when medical help arrived."

"A tray on a table wouldn't have made a difference." Lyle's congenial tone had vanished.

Sara raised her chin. "I'd planned to pull the table away, but didn't want to accidently cause the pie tray to topple to the ground."

Was she afraid if it had fallen cyanide might have touched her or someone else? Mary still couldn't get a good read on this woman. She wanted her to be guilty, but it was clear from her perspective that Sara had no motive.

"I see. Do you have any reason to want the sheriff dead?"

Sara gasped. "I most certainly do not, and I don't appreciate your questions. Unless you're arresting me, I'm leaving." She stood.

And there was the moxie that enabled the woman to be a success with her business. Mary didn't think she had it in her, but anyone who stood up to Lyle was either stupid or had guts—Mrs. McGovern wasn't stupid. Mary walked out of the room and slipped into her office. She'd heard enough.

A short while later, Lyle stepped into her office and closed the door behind him. He eased into a chair. "Well, that didn't go like I thought it would. She has a lot more spunk than I expected."

"I noticed. Do you like her for the murder?" Mary would be surprised if he said yes, but maybe he caught something she hadn't.

"I don't know. I would have said no before talking with her, but there's fire behind that drab exterior."

"Do you think she's not telling you something? Maybe her persona is all an act to help her blend in and not be noticed."

"It's possible." He sat back and rested his ankle on his knee. "She's smart and quick. I think she's capable, but I'm not convinced she's our killer."

"Then keep digging until you're convinced one way or the other. I don't need to tell you this person must be found and brought to justice ASAP."

"No, you don't." His gaze rested on her.

"What?" She hated it when he looked at her like he was trying to read her mind.

"I really want her to be the murderer."

"Me too. But?"

He hesitated then sat up and planted both feet on the floor. "She doesn't have a motive. I ran a background check on her, and she doesn't have so much as a parking ticket. She's had no reason to ever have had contact with you or anyone in law enforcement."

"No relatives behind bars?"

He shook his head. "She's spotless. An upstanding citizen."

"I realize we tend to be jaded, but perhaps in this case what we see really is the truth. She simply was trying to help by removing the tray and clearing the area for the medics."

"Maybe, but I'm going to keep digging to be sure. Right now she's our best lead."

"What about Albert Dunnigan? I read in your

report that May suspected him."

He shook his head. "He, nor his wife, were in attendance. They had a falling out with one of the other contestants and didn't want to be there."

"Do we know who they were avoiding?"

"Philomena Cartwright."

Now that was intriguing. Mary leaned forward resting her arms on her desk. "Tell me more."

"She made a disparaging remark about them to someone, and it got back to them."

"Figures. Philomena has probably alienated half the town with her sharp tongue. She's not my favorite person either. She spoke with me right before I was ready to judge."

Lyle raised a brow. "And?"

Mary pressed her lips together. Did the woman hate her enough to try and kill her? From her perspective, one would need a chainsaw to cut through the tension between them, but Philomena seemed to thrive on conflict. "I wouldn't put it past her. You know we have history."

"I'm aware."

"Have you questioned Philomena yet?"

He winced. "I had hoped to avoid her. She's a piece of work, but that doesn't make her a murderer."

"Due diligence, Lyle. Send Carter to talk with her."

"Do you really think she would try and kill you?" Doubt rested on his face.

"I wouldn't put anything past that woman, but no, probably not."

"Then why put Carter through that?"

"Like I said, due diligence." Plus it would be good

practice for Carter if he should win the election. Handling the Philomenas of the world would be like a nagging pain in his side he'd want to ignore but couldn't. He needed to learn how to deal with people like her if he was going to make a good sheriff. She shook her head—she wasn't giving up and needed to stop thinking as though she'd lost the election.

Lyle stood. "It's Sunday afternoon. Neither of us is on the clock. Want to take a walk in the park?"

She tilted her head to the side. Lyle had to be one of the most handsome men she'd ever met. His broad shoulders and strong arms a testament to his daily workouts. She would love to stroll in the park with him, but if they were seen together on a casual walk, wouldn't that get tongues wagging? The last thing she needed was to be the topic of yet another conversation. Goodness, she'd made the front page of the paper twice already in the past two weeks.

"Mary?" Questions filled his eyes. "Are you feeling too weak for that? We could go for a drive instead."

"I'm feeling a lot better. But people will talk."

"It's only a walk in the park."

She stood. There was no reason she shouldn't take a walk with a long-time friend. "Forget what people say. I'd love to get some fresh air and exercise with you. It's too beautiful of a day to be in this dungeon when I don't have to be." She scooted around her desk. "Let's go."

His face broke into a wide smile as he opened the office door. "After you."

"Thanks." She strode out the door all business. Strolling in the park was one thing, but when they were at work they would be strictly professional.

Lyle slipped on dark sunglasses. The hot sunshine beat down on his back, making him rethink his suggestion of a walk in the park.

"I wish I was wearing shorts." She fanned her face then laughed.

"What's so funny?" He grinned, reveling in her humorous mood.

"I've been freezing ever since my heart attack."

"Maybe your body has turned a corner and you're on the mend." He sure hoped so. He hadn't wanted to think about how weak she had looked. Today she appeared the strongest he'd seen her in days.

"I think you're right. I even feel more like myself."

"Praise the Lord." His insides bubbled with joy for Mary. He'd been so concerned for her. If she was on the mend, he'd feel much better about her being alone when she decided to go back to her place. Plus, she'd insisted she would return to work tomorrow and not simply camp out in her office. Her doctor had signed off on the medical release with the stipulation that she listen to her body. As if Mary would. He'd have to make sure she did. "Want to sit in the shade? Unlike you, I haven't been cold for days, and I'm roasting."

"Sure. I don't mind sitting." She stepped off the paved path and headed toward a stand of trees with several benches and picnic tables scattered throughout the treed area.

His hand brushed hers and a tingle zipped up his arm. He altered his course slightly so that wouldn't happen again. She'd made it clear that they were to remain friends, and though he didn't want to, he would respect her wishes.

She stopped at the first bench. "How's this one?"

Half the bench was in the sun the other half in the shade. "You don't need a little shade?"

"No. I've been sunning myself all week and rather enjoyed it. I credit my speedy recovery to all the extra vitamin D." She sat on the sunny side of the bench.

A breeze cooled him as he sat beside her. He glanced her way and noted her healthy glow. "I suspect you're correct about the vitamin D. You look beautiful." He cleared his throat. He tipped his head to the side, watching her reaction closely. Although he couldn't be certain since her face was already flushed, it looked as though her face had reddened slightly.

Hmm. It appeared he'd embarrassed her. Interesting. He didn't recall having done that before. "You up for a cold treat?"

"Maybe. What'd you have in mind?"

"Iced coffee."

"I could be persuaded."

He stood and held out his hand.

She looked around then slipped her hand into his. "Don't get used to this."

He chuckled. "Wouldn't dream of it." He laced his fingers with hers and breathed in a sigh of contentment. He'd waited so many years for a moment like this one.

She slid her fingers from his as soon as their feet touched the paved path. "We'll need to have a talk once we catch whoever is trying to kill me."

"A talk?" He glanced her way.

"About us."

"Us?" His heart pounded against his chest. Dare he hope she meant what he thought she was saying?

"Yes." A smile lit her eyes. "In the meantime, let's keep our focus on the prize—catching the bad guy."

"Not that I needed any more motivation to find this person, but the stakes are higher now."

She chuckled.

He opened the door to Roaster's Coffee for her. "After you."

"Thanks."

They stepped inside and cool air washed over them. He breathed in the scent of rich coffee as they headed for the cash register. "Afternoon, Pepper."

"Hey, Lyle." She looked at Mary. "Sheriff. What can I get for you?"

"Two large iced coffees please." He handed her a ten then stuffed a dollar into the tip jar. "Kind of quiet in here."

Pepper turned to prepare their drinks. "Yeah. Sunday afternoons are a little slow—especially in the summer. I should probably close on Sundays and let the drive-up coffee shack handle the morning rush, but this place is more my home than my home is. I'm not sure what I'd do if I had a day off."

"Maybe you should find out," Mary said. "Life is too short to spend it working all the time."

"I know you're right." Pepper placed their drinks onto the counter. "But it's easier said than done. For example, what if my customers like the drive-up better and stop coming here?"

"They'll be back. You can't recreate the ambiance of this place while sitting in your car." Mary picked up their drinks and handed one to Lyle. "Have faith in your business."

Pepper's face brightened. "It might be nice to have a life outside of here. Thanks. I'll consider what you said." She turned and wiped down the espresso machine.

"Are you closing?" Lyle asked.

"There's no better time than the present to try taking some time off."

Mary raised her cup toward Pepper. "Good for you. Lyle and I will flip the sign to closed, then scram."

"You don't have to do that. Have a seat. It will take me a bit to get things cleaned up."

"Which you will never do if you don't get that closed sign in place and lock up." Lyle headed for the door with Mary beside him. "Enjoy the sunshine." He'd always liked and admired Mary, but today he'd seen a side to her she rarely showed and his heart warmed like a gooey cinnamon roll. Ugh, what was happening to him? He was getting soft. Mary had that effect on him.

"Where to now?" Mary asked.

"Back to your office? I'm sure you're tired."

"As much as I hate to admit it, I am ready for a nap. But take me home, please. I miss my bed."

He'd wondered how long she'd last staying in her office. He glanced at the coffee in her hand. "If you drink that you'll be wired."

She shrugged. "I'll stick it in the fridge for tomorrow. Thanks, by the way."

"You're welcome."

"I need to go to my house for a few things. Do you

mind dropping me there instead?"

"Not at all." He guided them to his old Ford pickup then took Mary to her home. "I can take you back to the department when you're ready."

"That won't be necessary. I plan to hang out there for a little while, then I'll get Nancy to take me." Mary opened the door to his pickup and slid out. "Thanks for the ride. I really need a new car soon. I can't keep depending on other people to chauffeur me around town."

"I don't mind. I'm happy to wait around for you. I'm not crazy about you being here alone."

"I appreciate the concern, but last I checked I was still the sheriff. I can take care of myself."

He nodded. "I'll give you a lift in the morning. I have this coming Friday off. How about we shop then?"

"I work."

He shrugged. "We'll figure something out. Text me once you clear the place." He knew better than to insist she allow him to do it. He learned that lesson the last time he offered. He waited for her text then drove off. He still needed to find the Erika who owned the wig. His gut said she was key in solving this case, and locating her was now his top priority.

Chapter Fifteen

Monday afternoon Nancy listened to Laura read to a group of elementary-aged children. She sure had a way with them. Laura even did the voices of the different characters.

Her mind wandered to her talk with Carter last night. He'd confessed that though he'd wanted to start a family, the timing was off due to the election. She didn't agree, but was in no rush—at least not yet. The more she'd thought about it, the more she realized she could have kids and still consult with the sheriff's department. The idea of little ones depending on her was daunting, but she'd warmed to the idea.

Nancy's phone vibrated in her pocket. She stood and walked away from the reading circle. "What's up, Lyle. Is everything okay with my mom?"

"Far as I know. I'm calling because I found the Erika who bought the wig."

Nancy's insides leaped. "That's great news."

"Don't get too excited. Erika threw the wig away after getting frustrated with the fit. Remember that spot that didn't lay right?"

"Oh." Nancy leaned against the wall. Now what? "Did you ask her where she tossed it out?"

"And this is why you're good at this. She works at Best Little Burgers."

"BLB? She was right under our noses this entire time."

"Yep. She tossed the wig into the dumpster there."

Nancy pushed off from the wall and paced to the end of the hall. "You're kidding. Do they have surveillance cameras in their alley?"

"Affirmative. But I have hours of footage to wade through. Erika doesn't remember the exact day she tossed it. Only that she'd had an especially rough shift, and some girls from the high school had made fun of the wig."

"Erika's in high school?" Somehow she couldn't imagine a young woman wearing that wig, but clearly she'd been wrong.

"No. She graduated a couple of years ago. She had gotten a really bad haircut and thought the wig was cute—her words not mine."

Nancy grinned. As if a man couldn't use the word cute. "Okay. Did she happen to narrow down the week?"

"Yes, ma'am. I was hoping you could come over and help look through the footage. Your mom is here too."

Nancy's shoulder's sagged. "I wish I could. I've taken too much time off lately so I need to stay here. Can you send it to me?"

"Sorry, no. What about coming over after work?"

She had a standing engagement to walk with Anna. She'd understand, but she hated to change their plan. "I'll see what I can do. I might be able to burn the midnight oil and come in late."

"Sounds good. In the meantime, we'll keep at it and let you know if we discover who took it from the dumpster."

"Okay. Thanks for the call." She stuffed her phone into her pocket. They finally had a viable lead.

The rest of the afternoon dragged while her anxiety mounted. What if whoever took the wig had avoided the camera? Then again, why would they even try? They had no way of knowing they'd find a wig in the dumpster. Whoever went dumpster diving there was more than likely a homeless person looking for food. But if that was the case, how did the perp get the wig?

Laura and her daughter strolled over to the circulation desk hand-in-hand. "We're headed out. See you tomorrow."

Nancy stood. She'd been so lost in thought she hadn't realized the time. "I'll walk out with you." She shut down the computer and printer then grabbed her bag. "The story time went well. The kids were really into it." She walked with them toward the sliding doors.

"Doesn't it normally go well?" Concern filled Laura's voice.

"I think it always goes well, but you even had me engaged today, until I was interrupted with a phone call."

Laura nodded. "You've seemed distracted ever since that call. Is everything okay with your mom?"

"Yes. She's recovering well. Thanks for asking." Nancy turned and locked the doors. "See you tomorrow."

Laura waved and Clair skipped beside her.

Not for the first time, gratitude for her library assistant filled Nancy. Laura was the best. She shot off a text to her mom.

Any luck with the surveillance video?
Call me.

Nancy's heart skipped a beat. She yanked her phone from her pocket and made the call.

"That was quick," Mom said.

"You told me to call. What do you know?"

"A homeless woman took the wig."

"Anyone you recognize?"

"Maybe. We're looking for her now. She doesn't fit the profile of the person seen breaking into my home though."

"I didn't figure she would. Someone got that wig from her."

"That's my thought too. But we're a step closer."

Nancy unlocked her car and got in. A letter with her name on it sat on the front seat. "Mom, someone left a note on the front passenger seat. Do you know if Carter did it?"

"I don't. You think someone broke in?"

"It's possible. This car is a classic, and it's easy to pop the locks."

"Call Carter. He's canvasing for the homeless woman. If he didn't leave it, then I'll send someone over there to check it out and dust for prints."

"Okay." Unsettled, she placed the call to her husband. "Hey, there. You didn't happen to leave an envelope on my car seat, did you?"

"I didn't. But maybe Gavin did. He has a key to the car too."

"It's not his writing." It wasn't Carter's either, but she'd hoped it had been him. "I'll check to be certain."

"Hey. You've been careful, right? No one knows you're assisting in our investigation?"

"Only Anna." Her friend would never betray her.

"Okay. Give Gavin a call and let me know."

Five minutes later she had full-blown nausea. Neither Gavin nor Carter had left the envelope. That meant someone had broken into her car. She let Mom know. It looked like she'd have to alter her plans for this evening after all. With a sigh she went and sat on the steps that led up to the library door to wait for law enforcement.

Maybe the note was innocent. Or maybe it was a distraction to draw her attention from something explosive—like a bomb. Her heart rate accelerated as her imagination soared.

Nancy shook off the idea of a bomb. From where she sat, she couldn't see anything attached to the undercarriage. She'd left the window cracked—enough that someone could have slid the envelope in that way. But the chances of it floating down and landing so perfectly on the seat were slim.

A short while later Deputy Jacobson pulled to a stop behind her car. Nancy stood. "Hi, Brett."

"I hear you found a little trouble." He slipped on blue gloves and opened the driver's side door. He reached inside and pulled out the envelope. His brow wrinkled and a grim look settled on his face. He dropped it into an evidence bag.

"What are you doing?" She walked over to him and watched him work. If memory served, he'd been a deputy for about six years. She wondered how the election was affecting him. Would he resent having Carter as his boss if he won?

"Collecting the evidence."

"But I want to see what it says."

"You can later." The stern look on his face brooked no argument.

Something was definitely eating at the deputy. Had she done something or was his mood about something else? "Okay. How've you been?" Nancy asked. "I don't see you around much."

"Staying out of trouble. Which can't be said for you by the look of it."

"That wasn't very nice." What was up with him today?

"Calling it how I see it."

Nancy crossed her arms. "Is everything okay with you?"

He glared at her. "You going to tattle on me to your mom?"

She crossed her arms. "What are you talking about? First off, I never tattle, and number two, what would I tattle about if I did? What's going on?"

He shook his head and his face softened slightly. "Sorry. Bad day. I didn't mean to take it out on you." He looked off into the distance. "Some days I wish I'd chosen a different profession."

"And today is one of those days?"

"You got that right." His shoulders sagged ever so slightly.

"Are you sure I can't peek inside the envelope?"

"You can see it at the station once it's been processed. Like I said, it's evidence."

"Of what?"

"Someone breaking into your car."

She resisted rolling her eyes. "Okay." It seemed ridiculous to be so stringent, but he was already uptight, and if he wanted to follow the rules then she'd keep her mouth shut and let him. "I understand. Thanks for getting here so quickly. I might still be able to get in my walk with Anna."

He ignored her comment as he got into his cruiser and drove off.

Her gaze followed his vehicle. Had a bad day really been all there was to his attitude or had it been something else? Regardless of whatever was eating at the deputy, she aimed to find out what was in that envelope. She got into her car then paused. He hadn't dusted her car for prints.

Lyle bent his head, resting his elbows on his desk and rubbing his neck. Eight hours staring at a computer screen had left him sore. At least there was still a trail to follow.

Carter entered the bullpen. "I found her."

For the first time all day, Lyle let himself smile. He stood and accompanied Carter to the sheriff's office and closed the door. They each took a seat.

She looked up from a stack of paperwork. "I hope the expressions on your faces mean you bring good news."

"The best." Carter's leg bounced. "I found the woman in the video. Her name is Sadie."

"Sadie who?" Mary asked.

"She didn't have any ID and refused to tell me her last name. I doubt Sadie is even her name. Anyway, she said a woman approached her and offered her ten dollars for the wig."

"Who?" Lyle asked.

"She didn't know her. But said she wasn't very

big and had blonde hair."

"That narrows it down," Mary said, "but it's not what I'd hoped for. What about her age?"

"Unknown."

Lyle sighed.

"Hey," Carter said. "This is a step in the right direction. The trail hasn't run dry."

"Good point." Renewed energy surged through Lyle. "I'm going to go back through our persons of interest and see if any of them match this description."

A rap on the office door sounded. Lyle stood and pulled it open. "Nancy. Come in."

Her face lit when her gaze landed on her husband. She stood beside him. "What's the news?"

Carter filled her in. "I realize it's not a solid lead, but it's more than we had."

"I guess that rules out Philomena," Mary said.

Nancy wrinkled her nose. "I wouldn't do that yet. Sadie said the woman wasn't big. Philomena isn't either and in the right lighting, her hair could be mistaken for a shade of blonde." She rested a hand on Carter's shoulder. "How reliable is Sadie? Does she have all her faculties?"

"She was a little out of it at first. I bought her a meal and we talked quite a while. She seemed certain about what she told me."

Nancy pursed her lips.

Mary's eyes narrowed. "What are you thinking, Nancy?"

"I'm noodling some thoughts."

Lyle would have offered his seat, but knew Nancy thought best when in motion.

"What's to say this blonde woman who bought the wig wasn't already wearing one?"

Mary sucked in a breath. "I hadn't thought of that. Then the only real clue we have is the woman isn't big."

Carter cleared his throat. "Umm, Sadie was as tall as me. I imagine anyone shorter than her might fit that description."

Lyle shifted in his seat and blew out a long slow breath.

"I know my suggestion is discouraging, but the woman could as easily have had blonde hair."

Lyle appreciated her attempt to be positive, but there was no way to be certain Sadie had shared her own version of reality with Carter. "This is frustrating."

Mary's concerned eyes met his. "Don't you dare get discouraged. We are going to find this woman. However, I think we're probably safe to rule out Philomena."

Lyle nodded once. He had come to the same conclusion. The two women had history, but not the kind one committed murder for.

Nancy sat on the edge of her mom's desk. "Will one of you retrieve the envelope found in my car from evidence? Deputy Jacobson confiscated it. He also neglected to dust my vehicle for prints. I would have thought he'd have done that."

Mary's brows rose. "Brett's had a difficult day, but that's no excuse for sloppy work." She stood. "Where's your car?"

"I left it at the library and walked."

"Okay. Be right back."

Lyle waited until she left the room and closed the door. "I'd like to hear about this envelope, but first, what else do you know about this homeless woman, Carter?"

Carter frowned. "Sadie suffers from malnutrition. I have no idea if what she told me is reliable."

"Was anyone with her when she sold the wig?" Lyle asked. "Having someone corroborate her story would be helpful."

"I'll find out." He focused on Nancy. "I take it Gavin didn't leave the envelope?"

She shook her head. "I wish he had."

"Me too," Carter said.

"Tell me about this envelope." Why was he the last to know about whatever was going on?

Nancy explained what she'd found and how Deputy Jacobson insisted on entering it into evidence.

He frowned. "I wonder who could have left it?"

Nancy shrugged. "I'm more curious about what's inside."

The door opened and Mary strode in. She handed the envelope to Nancy. "It's okay to touch it now. Go ahead and look inside."

Nancy took it from her mom, noting it had already been opened. She pulled out a photo.

Lyle stood to get a better look at the photograph and his gut clenched. A picture taken of Stan, lying dead in the tent at the fair had the words "butt out or you'll be next" written across it.

Nancy frowned. "How? I've been so careful. No one should know I'm helping with this case except all of you and Anna. Why do the bad guys always think threatening me will get me to back off? As if." She tossed the photo onto Mary's desk.

Mary picked up the picture and studied it. "Who would take this and why? Lyle, will you make sure this isn't a copy of one of our photos?" She handed it to him.

Lyle's gaze snagged Mary's. "You think one of our people did this?" How could she? The sheriff's department was a family and would never intentionally hurt one of their own. That poison had been intended for Mary—no one here would have done that. Would they?

"No, but I need to make sure no one here is involved."

"Understood." But what if someone here was behind the poisoning? Were they so desperate to get her out of office they couldn't risk waiting for the election?

Chapter Sixteen

Exhaustion overtook Mary to the point she wasn't sure she would make it to Carter's car. He'd offered her a ride to their place for dinner. Since she had yet to go car shopping, she accepted the offer. Now if only she could get her feet to move.

Carter grasped her arm. "Are you okay?" Concern filled his blue eyes. "You're pale and you look ready to drop." He eased her into the nearest chair.

Talk about embarrassing. "I think perhaps I overdid it today."

"Perhaps?" he said sarcastically. "You and Nancy are so much alike. If either of you slowed down the earth would probably shift off its axis."

"Very funny. Will you get me a glass of cold water?"

"Sure. Be right back." He rushed away then returned a moment later with a cup. "Here you go."

She savored the cool water as it slid down her throat. She was probably dehydrated. She thrust the tiny cup at him. "More please."

His eyes widened. He took the cup and filled it without comment.

She took the cup from him when he returned and downed it in seconds. "Thank you. I needed that." More than she cared to admit. She had to take better care of herself if she wanted to get back to life as usual, and drinking plenty of liquids needed to move higher on her priority list. When had she last had anything to drink? Coffee at breakfast?

"Are you okay to walk now?"

She stood. "I think so."

"Good. You scared me."

"Sorry about that. I scared myself too. Let's get out of here." She was thankful Lyle had already left for the day. If he had witnessed that, he probably would have insisted on camping on her couch—though she didn't have a spare since she was still sleeping in her office. She was a bit of a mess tonight. Maybe she'd be better off moving back home. Surely she would get a better night's sleep in her own bed.

They finally made it to Carter's car, a black Dodge Dart. She collapsed into the seat and buckled in. Closing her eyes, she rested her head back.

Carter closed the driver's side door and a moment later the engine purred to life. "Are you sure you don't need medical attention?"

"No, but let's pretend I don't. Please take me home."

"No way. You're coming to our house. Nancy is expecting you for dinner. Besides, she'd have my head if I left you alone after that."

Her eyes popped open. "Nothing happened."

"Maybe not, but it could have."

She chuckled. "Could haves happen all the time, and you don't freak out."

"Maybe so, but you're my mother-in-law. I don't want anything to happen to you."

"That's probably the nicest thing you've ever said to me. You're not so bad yourself."

"Leave it to you to make light of this."

"You're welcome. Now take me home." She didn't bother to make sure he obeyed her command. Instead she closed her eyes. The next thing she remembered was strong arms slipping around her and then her soft bed. She rolled over as peace washed over her.

Lyle looked down at Mary as she slept, her face the picture of serenity. He owed Carter for calling him on his way to Mary's place. The poor guy didn't know what to do—take Mary to his place or take her home as ordered. According to Carter, she'd fallen asleep as soon as he'd pulled out of the parking lot.

Lyle brushed a hair away from her face and placed a soft kiss on her forehead. "Sleep well," he whispered then slipped from her bedroom and closed the door.

He'd camp out on her couch with Carter and Nancy's blessing. The town gossips were sure to spread rumors if his pickup spent the night out front, but what was he supposed to do? She clearly couldn't be alone, and her family had thought him staying was a good idea.

After making sure all the locks were secured, he stretched out on he couch and closed his eyes. Sleep evaded him. He sat up and pulled out the notepad he always carried even when off duty. He'd crosschecked the photo left for Nancy with the ones on file and it wasn't a match to any of the crime scene photos. Which meant the killer had been in the tent and taken a picture of Stan.

If Stan wasn't the intended target why take a picture? And why call out Nancy? He knew for a fact she was being careful. Who had she inadvertently tipped off and how?

Maybe he should be having this conversation with Nancy rather than himself. He wrote down his thoughts. He'd interview her first thing tomorrow. It seemed to him Nancy would be key in solving this case. Someone she came into contact with must be the murderer.

Unfortunately, narrowing down who that person was would be difficult, considering how many people Nancy saw on a given day working at the library. There was no way she would've given herself away there though. Could her phone have been hacked?

It seemed to him that was the most likely scenario. He shot off a text to Carter alerting him to his suspicion. His stomach churned from all the unanswered questions. Why hadn't the killer struck again after trying repeatedly to kill Mary? Had they accomplished their goal? They'd assumed the end game was to end her life, but what if it went deeper and the purpose was to make sure she didn't win the election?

Though she was still on the ballot, they all knew it would be close. Neither Carter nor Mary were campaigning anymore—an agreement they'd both come to. Would voting for Carter make him a traitor? He wanted to retire and wanted Mary to join him. But is that what she truly wanted? He knew she had feelings for him, but could she walk away from law enforcement?

Noise in the hall drew his attention. Mary padded into the living room.

"Hi."

She yelped and her hand reached for the sidearm that she wasn't carrying. Good thing he'd thought to remove it.

"It's only me." Lyle flipped on the lights even though he could see clearly in the dark with the light from the streetlamp shining in through the closed blinds.

"What are you doing here? You nearly gave me another heart attack."

"I'm sorry. Carter called me and said you insisted on staying at your place. He asked me to stay here since he had a special night planned for him and Nancy."

A look he couldn't quite identify rested on her face. "I was getting a glass of water. Would you like some?"

Somewhat taken aback at the change in subject, he stood. It wasn't like her to let something like this slide. "Sure. I can get it for us."

She nodded and eased into the closest chair.

Concern filled him as he quickly poured two glasses of water from the pitcher in the refrigerator. No wonder Carter wanted him here. She wasn't herself at all, and she clearly wasn't feeling well enough to defend herself against trouble.

He strode back into the living room and handed her a glass then returned to his spot on the couch. "Everything okay with you?"

She swallowed then rested the glass on her leg. "I overdid it today and neglected to drink enough."

He pressed his lips together. He never thought he'd hear the day she'd admit to overdoing it. A near death experience had a way of changing a person.

She'd been more mellow and reflective since her heart attack. Come to think of it, so had he.

"Are you okay with me being here?"

"Yes and no. Thank you for caring enough to stay."

"Of course. I'd do anything for you, Mary. You ought to know that."

She ducked her chin. "I think I do. But I don't want you to feel obligated."

"Never. I'm here because I care about you and want to make sure you're safe."

Silence hung in the air between them.

Mary tilted her head. "I'm not ready for the world to know how we feel about each other, but..."

He leaned forward. Could she be saying what he'd wanted to hear the last time they spoke like this?

"I'm ready for us to see where this"—she waved a hand between them—"goes."

Lyle tilted his head to the side. "Nancy has her heart set on us as a couple."

She chuckled. "My daughter has looked up to you since she was a little girl. Whether you realize it or not, you've been a father figure to her. But I'm not ready to bring her or anyone else into this yet. I'd like to keep *us* between us."

His heart tripped. He never expected to have this conversation tonight. It was almost more than his overly tired mind could handle. He needed to tread carefully and not say something stupid.

"You're quiet. Did I misunderstand your feelings for me?"

"Not at all. I'm in shock."

A soft grin rested on her face. "Then my work

here is done." She stood. "Sleep well." She padded from the room, leaving a shock wave in her wake.

Lyle closed his slackened jaw. What had just happened? He pinched his arm—yep he was awake. And probably would be for half the night after that declaration.

The following morning, Lyle scrambled eggs and toasted bread. He had the table set with coffee and juice along with their meal when Mary strolled out wearing her uniform. "Good morning."

"Morning yourself. You've been busy." She pointed to his clothes.

He looked down at his uniform. "I was up early and ran home to shower and change."

She sat at the table and breathed in deeply. "This smells amazing. I'm not sure I'm supposed to be eating like this though."

He grimaced. Scrambled eggs and toast were his morning staple. He'd had to go home and bring the eggs from his place before he could cook, so he probably should've figured it wasn't on her post heart-attack diet. "Is there something else you'd rather have?"

She grinned. "Absolutely not. One time isn't going to hurt." She sat down and bowed her head.

He offered a blessing over their meal then dug in. "How'd you sleep?"

"Very well. It helped knowing I didn't have to keep an ear out for trouble."

He nodded. He'd suspected she hadn't been sleeping for that very reason. "How about we go car shopping this coming weekend? I'm sorry we didn't get that done already."

"I'd like that and no worries. We were busy. Maybe by Saturday this case will be wrapped up. I've decided to move home. Sleeping on the couch in my office isn't working for me."

"Okay." Should he insist on camping out on her couch? He imagined she wouldn't go for the idea and chose to remain silent. "Any idea what kind of car you want?"

"I'd like to check out Volkswagen and Subaru."

He gulped down his orange juice. "SUV or car?"

"SUV. It's been a long time since I bought a vehicle, and I've secretly wanted a new one for quite a while."

He downed his coffee then pushed back from the table and took his dishes to the sink. "I'll get the dishes rinsed and into the dishwasher while you finish up." They had thirty minutes until their shift started.

Ten minutes later they were on their way. A pop sounded and his pickup swerved to the right. He fought the steering wheel.

"What happened?" Mary asked.

"Blew a tire I think." Or someone shot it out, but he hadn't heard a gunshot. Then again his tires were new and shouldn't have had a blowout. He stopped on the side of the road and looked around. "Maybe I hit something and it popped a tire." He climbed out, and sure enough, the front passenger tire was shredded. They were a few blocks from the courthouse. An easy walk for him, but Mary was another story.

He pulled out his cell and called for a tow. He wanted to have the tire checked to see why it had burst. He walked back to where it'd happened and didn't spot anything in the road.

Mary waited inside the pickup. A sign she still wasn't herself.

He strode over and opened the passenger door for her. "We should hoof it so we aren't late."

"What about your pickup?" She slid out.

"I called a tow. It'll be here soon." He checked his watch. They could still make it to work on time.

Mary's gaze kept a close eye on their surroundings. "Something doesn't feel right."

Alarm burned acid in his stomach. "You think this is a setup to get you in a vulnerable position?" The thought had crossed his mind as well.

"Anything is possible. When you were checking the tire, I called Nancy. She'll be here any minute."

At that moment, tires squealed as Nancy's Mustang careened around the corner. She skidded to a stop behind his truck, stuck her head out the window, and shouted, "Hop in."

"Looks like I need to have a talk with my daughter about the speed limit." She hustled to Nancy's car and slid into the front seat. She looked his way. "You coming?"

"I'll wait for the tow truck. See you soon."

"Suit yourself."

He waved as Nancy eased around his car and drove the speed limit. He imagined she'd get an earful from her mom, but he was thankful she hadn't wasted any time in getting here. There were too many unknowns to be certain of what had happened. His first priority was finding out what caused the blowout, then he'd interview Nancy.

Chapter Seventeen

"LYLE, YOU SHOULD KNOW BETTER THAN to ask me that." Nancy leaned against a wall of the bullpen where he had cornered her after she'd left her mom's office. "There is no way I would ever talk about that at the library where I could be overheard." *Unless...*

"What did you remember?" Lyle's eyes narrowed.

Nancy's face heated. "It wasn't my fault."

"Nancy," he drew out her name.

"Carter stopped in to see me at the library the Monday after the murder. He filled me in on some details of the case and my assistant might have overheard our conversation."

"Do you trust her?"

"I thought I did, but now I don't know." Nancy really didn't know that much about Laura. Her references had all checked out and she was exceptional at her job. "She's such a great mom. I have a difficult time entertaining the idea of Laura being a murderer."

"Given the right circumstances anyone is capable of anything."

She shook her head. "I choose to believe the best about her. She's a nice lady who has a gift with children. Kids wouldn't love her like they do if she was evil."

Lyle rubbed his chin. "You're probably right. But I'm still going to follow up with her. Did you discuss the case any place else in public?"

"Only on my walks with Anna, but there's never anyone around. Pepper might have brought up the murder while we were at her shop, but I don't remember for sure. Even if she did, I'm always super careful about what I say to her when it comes to this part of my life."

He nodded. "Did Carter tell you my suspicion about your phone?"

"I haven't spoken to him yet today. He was already out the door when Mom called, and I was in bed. Speaking of Carter, where is he? Shouldn't he be here?" It was only ten minutes after six in the morning so he should still be in the building.

"He's around."

She knew that much, but clearly Lyle wasn't going to reveal what her husband was up to. "What about my phone?"

"If you've been as careful as you say then the only other explanation I can come up with is your phone was hacked."

She wanted to toss her phone across the room at the idea someone could be spying on her. Instead, she thrust it at Lyle. "Can you get it looked at?"

"Of course. But I might need it for several hours."

"That's okay. If my phone is spying on me, I don't want to be anywhere near it." She couldn't get away from the sheriff's department fast enough. "I'm going to Roaster's then the library. If you get finished before the library opens, ring the bell at the back door, and I'll let you in."

She hustled from the bullpen and out to her car—she needed a chocolate donut. If someone really did hack her phone, she would need to change all her passwords, and who knew what else would be involved? She hoped and prayed Lyle was wrong and whoever had sent the picture had been on a digging expedition.

Now if that were the case, then the murder was likely someone who knew her. Someone aware that she consulted with the sheriff's department on non-violent type crimes. But this was far from a non-violent crime, so no one should suspect her of being involved. Except her mom was the target, and anyone who knew her would know she couldn't stay out of the investigation.

Even before she was officially brought onboard, she was sniffing around, trying to figure out who-dun-it. Her reputation as a sleuth could be her downfall with this case. Who did she know that had the nerve to kill someone and go on as if nothing happened?

She parked and headed into Roaster's behind May Wallace. "Good morning," Nancy said.

May looked over her shoulder and smiled. "Hi, Nancy. You're out early today." She faced forward and headed for the register.

Nancy followed. "Yeah. Where are you working today, May?"

"The Mayor's office. But it doesn't open for a while yet. I'm an early riser. Not that I ever really slept." She got in line ahead of Nancy and placed her order.

"You're still not sleeping well?" Nancy felt for the woman. Lack of sleep did crazy things to a person.

"No. I'm getting desperate for a solid night of z's." She placed her order. "I'll see you around."

"Sure. I hope you have a good day."

"You too." May walked to the pick up spot at the other end of the counter.

Nancy glanced around the coffee shop, which was surprisingly busy. Was that Daisy in the corner booth with Deputy Jacobson? Weird. She'd never noticed Daisy at any of the shops besides her diner and Nancy had lived in Tipton her entire life.

"This is a surprise."

Nancy turned back to face Pepper.

"Yeah." Normally she'd still be snug in bed.

Pepper eyed her. "What's wrong? You never come in this early."

"Mom needed me."

"You look like you rolled out of bed and threw on the first thing you could put your hands on."

Nancy frowned and looked down at her mismatched skirt and top. "Oops. Not exactly the put-together look I was hoping for." Maybe a trip home before work would be a good idea. "You're a keen observer, my friend. Could I have a coffee to go and a bacon and egg sandwich?" She wasn't in the mood to cook after being awakened so abruptly.

"Coming up."

Nancy paid then stood at the opposite end of the counter to pick up her order. So much for enjoying a relaxing cup of coffee. She had hoped to visit with Pepper.

Pepper handed Nancy her order. "Do you have to rush off? I could take ten."

Nancy eyed the clock. "I could spare ten minutes." She would simply have to make her trip home in record time. No big deal. The scolding her mom had given her about speeding and reckless driving tickled her brain, but it wasn't as if she drove like that all the time. That was an emergency.

Pepper dropped a teabag into a cup and filled it with hot water. "Let's grab a window seat before they're all gone." She led the way and sat. "What has you out and about so early?"

"Lyle had a blowout while he and Mom were headed to work. She called me to come and rescue them. Turned out only mom needed rescuing."

Pepper blew on her cup of tea then took a tentative sip. "I'm glad you stopped in." She looked over her shoulder and lowered her voice. "I've been doing some eavesdropping."

Coffee almost spewed from Nancy's mouth, but she stopped herself in time. "Go on." That her friend eavesdropped was no secret to her, but for Pepper to openly admit it was unexpected.

"A lot of folks come in here to meet up with friends, and well, they've been discussing the upcoming election."

Nancy exhaled a long slow breath. She'd temporarily forgotten about the election. "What are you hearing?"

"It's close, Nancy. I mean really close. I think this town could be split down the middle."

"More people than the residents of this town vote. Remember, it's a county-wide election."

"I know, but it's a good sampling of the pulse of the community."

Nancy nodded. It was no secret several farmers met here on a regular basis to have coffee with one another, so Pepper's observation really did extend beyond the town of Tipton and into the countryside.

Pepper's brow furrowed. "Would you be terribly upset if your mom lost the election?"

"Honestly, no. Which surprises me. But I really wish Carter wasn't the one running against her." It felt as though Mom was ready to leave office. Talk about a one-eighty from where she'd been a short time ago.

"You don't want him to be sheriff?" Pepper's brow furrowed.

"Not really, but for purely selfish reasons." She stared at her coffee then raised her head. "I know what a toll the job took on my mom. I don't want that for Carter. Plus, I want him to be with *me*, not working all the time." She shrugged. "If he wins, I'll get over it and support him."

Pepper motioned toward her untouched sandwich. "Are you going to eat that before it gets cold?"

Nancy unwrapped her breakfast. "Yes, sorry." She bit into it and grinned. "Delicious." She quickly ate and washed it down with coffee while Pepper silently sipped her tea, allowing her to focus on eating versus talking. She popped the last bite into her mouth.

Pepper looked over her shoulder then motioned Nancy to lean in. "There are some folks talking about you and your mom. They said they were surprised you hadn't yet figured out who poisoned Stan since it was intended for your mother."

Nancy gasped. "What makes them think I'm on that case?"

Pepper gave her a look that said 'you're kidding.' "You wouldn't be you if you didn't get involved. After all, we are talking about your mom."

Nancy pressed her lips together. "Can I get a chocolate donut to go please?" She should have ordered it to begin with, considering it was the reason she'd come in to begin with. She was definitely off her game this morning.

"Of course. I didn't mean to stress you out."

"You didn't. I actually came in to buy one." She paid Pepper for the donut and headed out to her car, keeping a close eye on her surroundings. Unease gripped her as she got into her car. Was someone watching her? She looked around and didn't notice anyone suspicious. She started her car and headed home to make herself presentable for work.

Later that night, Nancy sat at her kitchen table with her laptop, running through the surveillance from Mom's neighbors. Lyle had returned her phone as she left the library. It hadn't been compromised, so they were no closer to figuring out how anyone knew she was involved with the case. Maybe it was the town gossip that had prompted the threat.

Gavin sauntered into the house, carrying his skateboard. "Hey, Nancy."

"Hey, yourself. How's it going?"

"Fine."

"How's Maddie?"

He stopped and looked in her direction. "Fine?"

"You don't know?" This was exactly what she'd been afraid would happen. "School starts on Tuesday. Haven't the two of you talked?"

"I've been busy." His gaze shifted away from her.

"With Ciara?"

"Why the third degree?" He snapped. He moved toward the hall.

"Please don't use that tone with me."

His shoulders drooped. "Sorry."

"Thank you." Gavin had been testy off and on lately, but from what she'd gathered from Carter, he went through phases like this. "Anna is concerned about Maddie."

Gavin stilled and turned to face her. "What's wrong with Maddie?"

"I don't know. That's why I asked you since you're her best friend."

He frowned. "I haven't talked with her for a few days. Ciara and I have been busy."

"Hmm."

"What's that supposed to mean?" He sounded annoyed again.

"It was a simple hmm. Don't try and read into it, Gavin. But I think you should give Maddie a call. She could be feeling left out if you've been spending all your time with Ciara and not including her."

He came back to the table and plopped onto a kitchen chair with a sigh. "I really like Ciara."

"I'm happy for you, but that shouldn't change anything with Maddie."

"Ciara doesn't like Maddie."

Nancy's head jerked. "Come again? I thought they were friends. That's why Maddie set the two of you up."

His necked reddened. "Ciara used Maddie to get my attention."

Nancy blew out a breath and closed her laptop. "I

didn't see that coming."

"Me neither. I don't know what to do. I really like Ciara."

"In spite of the fact she was cruel to your best friend and used her and deceived you in the process?"

"Forget it. You don't understand." He tried to stand.

Nancy stopped him with a hand on his arm. "Don't go. I'm sorry. I've never met Ciara. I'm sure she has many good qualities. But answer me this. Are you willing to throw away your friendship with Maddie to be with Ciara? Is she worth it?"

"I'm home," Carter said. He walked into the kitchen. "How are my two favorite people?" He cupped her shoulder with his hand.

Nancy offered a weak smile and rested her hand over his. "We were having a talk about girls."

His gaze shot to Gavin. "What's going on?"

"Nothing." He left the room.

Nancy explained the situation to Carter.

Carter scrubbed his hands over his face. "What do we do?"

"I'm newer at this parenting thing than you are. I guess we let him handle it."

"I feel badly for Maddie. Does she know Ciara used her like that?"

"If she hasn't figured it out yet, I'm sure she will soon." Nancy rested her hand on his knee. "I think this is one of those things we need to turn over to the Lord. I've said what I needed to say to him. I'm sure he knows what he should do."

Carter nodded. "Okay. Moving on." He motioned toward her laptop. "What were you working on?"

"The surveillance video from my mom's neighbor. There's something familiar about the person who broke in, but I can't put my finger on it."

"Don't give up. You'll figure it out." He stood and pulled her into his arms. "I've missed you."

"I didn't go anywhere." She murmured between kisses.

He nuzzled her neck. "I enjoyed last night."

Her thoughts shifted to the spontaneous romantic evening they'd had.

"What do you say when this is all over we go away for a weekend?"

"I'd love that, but what about Gavin?"

"He can stay with your mom."

Nancy chuckled at the idea. "I'd love to be a fly on the wall *that* weekend." Mom's no-nonsense approach to parenting might give Gavin whiplash.

Chapter Eighteen

Early Saturday afternoon, Lyle drove to Salem with Mary in the passenger seat. "Are you excited about buying a car?"

"That's a loaded question." She chuckled. "Let's just say, I'm excited to finally have my own transportation again. At least I hope I find something. I'd be really disappointed if I can't make a good deal today."

"I'm sure you'll find something. When we're done, how about we catch a movie and dinner?"

"As in a date?" Caution tinged her voice.

He gripped the steering wheel tight. "As in exactly a date. We'll be out of Tipton, away from prying eyes, so I thought..." He glanced in her direction. "Your heart attack woke me up to the fact we are wasting time. There is no legit reason you and I can't follow our hearts right now. We aren't kids. Let's not waste another day."

Her silence made his shoulders tight. Had she changed her mind since their talk the other night?

She cleared her throat. "I can't believe I'm agreeing about this, but you're absolutely right. We can still keep what's between us to ourselves. And if someone sees us there then so be it. We must find whoever is out to get me before the election, though, and we can't allow our relationship to get in the way."

"I agree, but why that timeline? Not that I expect

it to take that long."

"Several reasons. One, I don't want to leave office with that hanging over my head."

"You could win." Had she given up?

"Not if we don't catch this person. Besides that, I'm ready for a change."

"It seems we're in the same place."

"You want to retire too?" Surprise filled her voice.

"Have for a while." He glanced in his rearview mirror and frowned. A black economy-size car had been following them since they'd left Tipton. He changed lanes and signaled to turn right toward Independence.

"What are you doing?"

"We might have a tail, but it's hard to tell on the highway since we haven't come to any exits after leaving Tipton." Anyone who wanted to go to Independence wouldn't have taken the highway—it would have been the longer route from Tipton. Taking that turn would be the perfect way to know if someone was following them or not, since it was an unlikely route.

He slowed and turned then kept on the country road that would eventually lead to the small town. The black car followed. His pulse amped. "We have a tail."

Mary shifted and looked back. "Wish I had binoculars."

"Glove box."

He sensed her gaze on him and glanced her way. "What are you waiting for? Find out who's following us."

"Yes, sir." She pulled out the binoculars and held

them to her eyes. "You're not going to believe this."

"Oh, I think I might. Is it Brett?" Deputy Jacobson hadn't been himself.

"How'd you know?" She shifted to face forward.

"A hunch. I don't like him for Stan's murder. However, he might be mixed up with something else." He pulled over and stopped along the side of the road.

Brett kept driving.

"Now what?" Mary asked.

"We follow him." So much for car shopping and their date, but if his gut was right, tailing Brett would be worth the sacrifice.

Contrary to what Lyle thought, Mary couldn't shake that Brett Jacobson was in some way involved with Stan's murder, but she had no evidence to back it up. They'd followed him to downtown Independence where he'd parked and gone into a restaurant. She put down her window and looked at the restaurant. "What is he up to?"

"He's smart. He knows we spotted him following us." Lyle opened his door. "You coming?"

"What are you doing?" Did he really plan to confront Brett here? She got out.

"Thought we'd grab a bite to eat." He walked around the front of the pickup and offered her his arm.

She shook her head. "Thanks, but I'm not sure confronting him in a public place is a good idea. What if he's carrying? If this goes south, innocent people could be hurt or killed."

"I guarantee he's carrying, but I don't think we

need to worry about him doing something stupid. We're only going to have a friendly chat. Relax." He moved toward the entrance right as Brett walked out. Lyle stopped. "We were coming in to see you, but this is easier."

Brett's face hardened. He held a paper bag in his left hand. "I wasn't following you."

Yet that was the first thing he said to them without any accusations from them. Mary looked around. Good thing the sidewalks were mostly empty, except for a couple strolling hand in hand on the other side of the road.

"Sure looked that way to me," Lyle said. "Let's take a walk."

Brett glared but complied.

"Cut the crap. Why'd you follow us?" Lyle asked.

Brett blew out a breath. "I wanted to see where you were going?"

"Why?"

"Can we talk privately?"

Lyle crossed his arms. "No. If this involves the sheriff, she deserves to hear what you have to say."

Deputy Jacobson frowned. "Forget it." He started to walk away.

Lyle grabbed his arm. "We can talk here or in the interrogation room. Your choice."

"You have no reason to question me. I didn't break any laws."

Mary raised a brow. "You sure about that?" She softened her tone. Clearly the man had a problem with her. "Look, we want to understand what's going on with you. We aren't accusing you of anything except going way out of your way to come here. You have to admit, following us to that turn looked suspicious."

"I'm sure it did, but I wanted a change in scenery."

"Bull." Mary couldn't believe his lame excuse.

"Let's say we believe you," Lyle said. "What do you know about the murder of Stan Gibson?"

Pain crossed Brett's face. "Clearly you aren't going to let this go, and my lunch is getting cold. I think I know who poisoned the pie."

Mary's stomach flipped. "Why didn't you say anything?"

"Because I'm not sure. It's a hunch."

Lyle's forehead wrinkled. "We could've followed up on your hunch."

"But if she's innocent, I didn't want her reputation ruined."

Mary sighed. "I'm not worried about this woman's reputation. We need to investigate all possible leads. Why did you hold out on us?"

"She's a friend. If word got out that she's a suspect, it would destroy her. And don't say word wouldn't get out. We all know how the gossip train works in Tipton."

"She your girlfriend?" Lyle asked.

"No," Brett snapped. "But accusing her of murder would ruin her life."

"Her life? Don't you think that's an exaggeration?"

Brett raised his chin. "Absolutely not."

"Fine. We'll be discrete. Let us talk to her at a location of your choosing." Lyle rested a hand on the hood of his pickup.

"I can't," Brett said. "This is something I need to

do."

"Why?" Mary narrowed her eyes.

"Because she trusts me, and I don't want to destroy that trust."

"What's in the bag?" Lyle reached for it.

"I told you. My lunch." He thrust the bag at Lyle. "See for yourself."

Lyle looked inside and handed back the bag. "We aren't done talking about this. But we have a car to buy. See you later." He walked around to the driver's side and climbed in.

Mary's attention shifted to Brett. "Before your shift begins on Monday, I want to see you in my office."

He nodded. An angry glint shone in his eyes.

She got into the pickup and buckled in. "That was..."

"Odd?" He pulled out and did a U-turn so they'd be headed in the direction they'd come.

"Sure. Let's go with that." Who was the "she" Brett had been talking about? Maybe Carter or one of the other deputies would know. She'd have to tread carefully, so word wouldn't get back to Brett. "Let's forego car shopping. I'll get a rental."

"Are you sure?"

"Positive. Rain check on our date?"

"Of course. You didn't believe Brett, did you?"

"I think he's trying to protect someone, and I aim to find out who."

"What do you say we do it together?"

Her heart melted at the smile he sent her. "I won't pass up the help."

After taking Mary to a car rental company and following her back to town, Lyle headed downtown to meet Carter and Nancy. He pushed open the door into Daisy's diner. He spotted the couple along the back wall and headed their direction.

Kari, his usual waitress, spotted him and waved. "I'll be right over to take your order."

He nodded and continued toward Carter and Nancy. "Thanks for agreeing to meet on such short notice." He sat beside Carter.

"It sounded urgent," Carter said.

"I believe it could be." He motioned for them to lean close. In a hushed whisper, he filled them in on what had gone down with Brett earlier in the day.

Nancy's expression had turned from curious to disturbed as she took in his recounting of the events. "I noticed he was off the other day too. I guess now I know why. He's worried about someone he cares about." She propped her elbow on the table, resting her chin in the palm of her hand. "I wonder who it could be."

"Are you ready to order?" Kari asked.

They each ordered the special, then Kari walked away. Daisy's Diner was busy tonight so they should be able to finish their conversation without interruption.

Nancy's face lit.

"What did you remember?" Lyle asked, keeping his voice so quiet there was no way anyone at the tables around them would hear.

"I saw Deputy Jacobson the other morning with

Daisy in Roaster's," Nancy said.

Lyle's gaze shot toward the kitchen. "This Daisy? As in the owner of Daisy's Diner?" How many times had he and Mary eaten here of late? His stomach roiled at the idea she could be the murderer and could have easily taken both of them out.

Nancy nodded. "One and the same. I thought it was odd at the time, but if he has a thing for her, then that would explain why she was at Roaster's with him."

Why would Daisy want to kill Mary? He couldn't come up with a single reason, but Daisy's image had been in all the photos he had of the event.

Nancy's face paled. "Is it safe to eat here?" She kept her voice low.

"I don't think she'd risk her business by poisoning customers. Do you really think it's possible she's the murderer?" It didn't make sense to him that Daisy would want Mary dead.

Nancy shrugged. "I would be surprised, but I've been surprised before so..."

Carter reached for his water glass. "Before we do anything, let's think about this. Sure, Daisy had the means and opportunity, but what's her motive? Your mom is a good customer. We all are. There haven't been any issues here that I know about. Why would she want your mom dead?"

Exactly!

"Murder doesn't have to make sense," Nancy said.

Lyle nodded. "True, but I don't think she's a cold-blooded killer. If she did this, there would be a reason."

"Why not ask her?" Carter motioned toward the

kitchen.

Lyle shook his head. "Not here or now." Brett had been clear about not casting aspersions on the woman he was talking about. On top of that, they didn't even know if Daisy was that woman. They needed Brett to come clean with them.

"Why not?" Nancy frowned. "I'd think you'd want to solve this case ASAP."

"I do, but not at the detriment of an innocent person. We could ruin her business if people thought there was a chance she'd poisoned the pie that killed Stan." He would wait for Brett to confirm what they thought before acting on Nancy's information.

"But if we don't do something, and she really is the killer, another innocent person could be killed." Nancy pressed her lips tightly together as Kari approached with their meals.

"Three chicken specials." Kari set a plate piled with food in front of each of them. "Let me know if there's anything else I can get for you."

Lyle met her eyes. "We will. Thanks."

She smiled and headed to the next table over.

Lyle patted Nancy's hand. "Slow down. You're getting ahead of yourself. Remember, we don't know if she's the one Brett mentioned."

"I know, but who else could it be? I never see him out with anyone. Actually, I never see him out at all. Apparently, he works and spends his free time at home."

Carter speared a piece of chicken with his fork. "I'm with Lyle on this. We need to move forward with caution. So far everyone we've questioned had nothing to lose, but this is different. She's a community and business leader. We don't want to disparage her."

"Then we are in agreement. Nancy, you need to let us handle this," Lyle said.

"No problem. I don't want any bad blood between us. I like Daisy."

"We will try to avoid that." Lyle stood. "If either of you learn anything let me know. In the meantime, we can talk again on Monday after the library closes. Hopefully by then, your mom will have gotten Brett to talk." He dropped a twenty on the table and left. He'd come back at closing time to question Daisy.

Chapter Nineteen

Mary peered at Deputy Jacobson as he sat across from her in her office. "How are you, Brett?"

"I've been better. Aside from having my sleep schedule messed up, and well, you know."

But did she? "I'm not sure I do. You haven't been as forthcoming as I'd like. We want to talk with the woman you're concerned about."

He shook his head. "I said I'd handle it."

Mary took a breath and let it out, keeping her face neutral. "I understand wanting to protect someone you care about. It's a natural instinct, but if she is involved in Stan's murder we need to know."

"That's the issue, Sheriff. I don't know if she is or not, and I won't give you her name until I know for sure."

She respected his loyalty, but at the same time frustration consumed her. "I could hold you for impeding an investigation."

He closed his eyes and shook his head. After several deep breaths he opened his eyes. "It's May."

A jolt shot through her. "The mayor's daughter?" Why would May want her dead?

Pain etched on his face. He nodded.

"Why do you suspect her?"

"We are good friends. She fell hard for Stan last school year when she was filling in as the receptionist. That was before she got the post office job."

"I'm not following. If she loved him then why take that risk?"

"I'm not sure she did, but I know she could have had the know-how to make it but maybe not understand what she was messing with. She went to college to study biology. I'm not sure what happened, but she changed her major. I got the impression biology might have been more than she could manage."

Mary stilled. That was the lead they'd been waiting for—an amateur scientist might be able to unwittingly pull off a murder by poison. "Do you know where she's working today?"

"Not for sure, but I think the post office."

Mary blew out a breath. "Do you think she's dangerous?"

"Not to the public. She's a woman who wanted the man she loved to succeed at any cost."

"So you think she did it?" Mary's pulse thrummed in her ears.

"I hope she didn't. But yeah, it's a strong possibility."

"What about the note found in Nancy's car? Did she put it there?"

He frowned. "I can't say for certain, but the handwriting looked like it could be hers."

Mary stood. "Why didn't you tell me your suspicion then? My daughter could be in danger," her voice lowered as anger consumed her.

"Because I needed to be certain. It's a big deal to accuse the mayor's daughter of murder. We have no proof. No evidence at all leading to her. Only my suspicion."

Mary sat heavily into her chair. "I might be able to get a search warrant based on the letter she left for Nancy."

"*If* she left it. We have no proof."

"Did you ask her if she sent it?" Mary's patience was wearing thin.

"I did."

"And?"

"She denied it."

"Of course she did. We need a handwriting sample to compare it with. Think you could get that for us?"

"I'll try."

Nancy missed the meeting with her mom and the men about the case. She'd been delayed in closing the library and didn't want to keep Anna waiting. The idea of Daisy being a murderer ate at her all day. She kept thinking of the surveillance video of the person who broke into her mom's home. The body types didn't match. Which meant if Daisy was the killer, then she had an accomplice.

"That's it!" She stood and rushed to her laptop sitting on her kitchen table.

Anna followed. "What's going on?"

"Something's been bothering me about the surveillance video from the day of the break-in at my mom's place." She woke up her computer and pulled up the video. She pressed play and watched it for a few seconds then froze the screen. "Look. I hadn't realized it before."

"What am I looking at?" Anna bent down, studying the image on the screen.

"The person. Doesn't she look familiar?"

"I assumed it was a man. Granted a man of small stature, but still a man."

"And that's why no one thought of this before. I have a hunch."

"You know who is in the video?"

"I believe I do, but I have to prove it." The beginning of a plan began to percolate in her mind. "I'm going to need your help." She explained her idea to Anna.

Anna shook her head. "I don't believe it."

"Why not? She said herself she cared about Stan."

"Lots of people cared about him. I cared about him." Anna's eyes narrowed. "Do you think she wanted to assure he'd win the election by taking out the competition?"

"That's exactly what I think." She closed her laptop. "Let's go."

"Where?"

"To her house. We need to get her to confess."

Anna crossed her arms. "No way. You need to call Carter. Tell him your suspicion. Do this the right way."

Nancy sucked in a breath and let it out sharply. "Maybe so." After all, if her hunch was right, they'd be in the home of a killer who might be desperate enough to kill again. "Carter is still at work, so I'll text him."

Going to the mayor's house. I think May killed Stan.

Stop!

Nancy froze. Carter never used exclamation marks.

Why?

We are en route now. Stay clear of her place.

Nancy sighed.

"What's the matter?" Anna sidled up to her.

Nancy handed her the phone.

"They already figured it out, or they're acting on your tip?"

"I have no clue, but I'm guessing they figured it out." She frowned.

"What's the matter? This is a good thing. Right?"

"Yes. Of course, but I wanted to be there. I hate being left out."

Anna chuckled. "You have too much of a lust for adventure. If May is a killer, you don't want to have anything to do with her arrest. Do you think she's the one who sent that note?"

"No idea, but I'd say it's likely." She probably shouldn't have filled Anna in about the note left in her car, but she trusted Anna implicitly. "I'll make a pot of coffee. It might be a long night."

"None for me. I have to be at work bright and early tomorrow."

"That's right, I forgot school started this week. How's it going?"

"Like every other first week. Challenging."

Nancy nodded in understanding. "I imagine it would be." She glanced at her phone. When would Carter send her an update? As nervous as she was, coffee was probably a bad idea.

The front door slammed. "I'm home," Gavin said.

"In the kitchen." Nancy pulled enchiladas from the warming oven. "Dinner's ready."

He strode into the kitchen and pulled up short when he spotted Anna. "Oh, hi, Miss Plum."

"Hi, yourself. How's life?"

"Not bad."

"Senior year, right?"

"Yes." He grinned. "Dinner smells good." He went to the sink and washed his hands, then dished up a couple of enchiladas. "Where's Uncle Carter?"

"Working."

He pulled a cup from the cupboard and filled it with ice water then sat at the table with his meal. "He's been working a lot lately. Is this what it will be like if he wins the election?"

"Probably." Nancy joined him at the table.

"I'm going to head home." Anna mouthed "call me" to Nancy then left.

Nancy fiddled with a napkin. "Will you be okay with him not being around much if he wins the election?"

"I'm going away to college. It's going to affect you more than me. How do you feel about him becoming sheriff?"

"I'd rather he lose." She pressed her lips tight, uncertain how her blunt honesty would be accepted.

Gavin took a huge bite and chewed then washed it down with water. "I can see why. You were right about Maddie."

"Oh?"

"Yeah. Her feelings were really hurt. The more I thought about it, the more I realized I don't want a girlfriend that would treat my best friend like that."

"So you and Ciara are no longer together?"

"Nope."

"And how are things with Maddie?"

"Fine, I guess. She was pretty ticked at first, but when I told her I broke up with Ciara, she was fine again."

Nancy grinned. "I'm glad." One problem solved. One to go. She glanced at her phone again. When would Carter text?

Chapter Twenty

Lyle, with Carter by his side, rang the doorbell of the home of Mayor Wallace. The door swung open and he presented the mayor with a search warrant. "I'm sorry about this, Mayor," Lyle said. "We have reason to believe May is responsible for the death of Stan Gibson."

Charlie's face paled and he clung to the door for support. "There must be some mistake. May would never…"

Carter stepped past the mayor and gently guided him to the nearest chair. "I'm sure this has come as quite a shock, sir. Is your daughter home?"

"She's in the backyard reading a book."

Lyle strode for the sliders along the backside of the house. He stepped outside into the cool evening air. Crickets chirped signaling dusk. May sat on a lounger with a book in her hand. "It's going to be too dark soon to see that."

May gasped and looked up. "What are you doing back here? You can't barge in like this."

"Your Dad let us in."

"Us?"

"Yes. Deputy Malone is in the process of searching your home." He handed her the search warrant and watched as she read the contents.

Her breath came in short gasps and tears slid down her cheeks. "It was an accident."

"What was?"

"I never meant to kill Stan. I must have done my math wrong when I was adding the cyanide. It was only intended to make the Sheriff sick so she would pull out of the race. I guess I messed up or made the wrong kind or...I don't know what happened," her voice cracked.

"You didn't think Stan could beat her on his own?"

She hiccupped and shook her head. "I've felt so horrible. It's almost a relief to have the truth out. What's going to happen now?"

"If you cooperate, it will all go very smoothly."

"Got it." Carter stood in the doorway to the house, holding several evidence bags with bottles inside them.

Lyle read May her rights. Sadness consumed him as he cuffed the woman and guided her through her home.

Mayor Wallace stood. "Oh, May. What have you done?"

"I'm so sorry. I didn't mean to kill anyone. You have to believe me."

"Of course I do." He frowned. "Did you send me the email about giving the sheriff the first round of pies to taste?"

She nodded. "Will you find an attorney for me?"

"Right away. Don't say anything more until you have representation."

"Okay." She raised her shoulder and wiped her tear-streaked face on her filmy blouse.

An hour later, Lyle sank into Mary's sofa and pulled her close. "It's finally over. May is behind bars and you're safe."

"Did she say why she came after me again after her first attempt failed? It seems odd that she'd try to poison me again when her only reason for trying to harm me in the first place was to get me out of the race."

"I asked her about that on the way to the station, and she wouldn't talk. Perhaps she wanted to stop you from investigating. Or maybe her mistake made her angry, and she blamed you. It's hard to know why people do the things they do."

Mary rested her head on his shoulder. "True. I suppose we may never understand. Thank you for taking over and making the arrest."

He kissed the top of her head. "You're welcome. I know you wanted to be involved."

"I did, but I realized me staying out of the way was for the best. I appreciate your wisdom on that."

He grinned. "You know what I appreciate?"

"Hmm?"

"That you and I can focus on us now rather than finding Stan's killer."

"Until the next big case."

He chuckled. "This is Tipton."

"Exactly."

He shook his head. They'd had more than their fair share of criminal activity in Tipton County, but he had to believe things would get better—probably the optimist in him. "Now that the case is over, I owe you a date. What do you say?"

She tipped her head back, grinning. "I'd say absolutely."

Lost in the depths of her deep brown eyes he drew closer and found her soft lips.

Epilogue

NANCY BREATHED IN THE SCENT OF cinnamon rolls. Pepper had offered to host an election results party at Roaster's Coffee. By the smell of things, she'd spent extra time in the kitchen baking today. "Pepper, you are the best friend a girl could ask for. Thanks for offering to do this here. We probably all would have gathered at my place or my mom's otherwise."

"It's my pleasure. I'm not one for politics but seeing as both candidates are related to my best friend, this seemed like a good idea."

Anna walked over to them, holding a plate containing a warm and gooey cinnamon roll. "These are amazing, Pepper. Why don't you have them on your menu?"

Pepper grinned. "Thanks. I only sell them once a year on Christmas Eve."

"Well, put me down for six. Luke and Maddie would love these," Anna said.

"Speaking of those two, where are they?" Nancy looked around the coffee shop. "I thought they were coming."

"They'll be here in a bit. Maddie was finishing up her math homework when I checked on them. You know Luke, no fun and games until all the work is done."

Nancy nodded. "That sounds about right."

The door to the shop jingled announcing more attendees.

Anna grinned wide. "And there they are. At least they didn't miss the announcement. Excuse me." She greeted her fiancé and soon to be stepdaughter a few feet inside the door.

"When do you think they will make the call about who won?" Nancy asked.

Pepper shrugged. "I have no idea, but I'm guessing soon. I need to check on something in the kitchen."

"Sure." Nancy moved over to a table where Mom and Carter talked in hushed tones. "What's going on? Are the two of you planning something?"

"In a way." Carter tugged her into his lap.

He knew she was uncomfortable with public displays of affection, but close friends surrounded them so she did her best to relax and enjoy the moment. "How much longer?"

"Should be any time now," Mom said.

Since Oregon did mail-in ballots they'd know tonight who won the election. "I'm so nervous." Nancy stood, unable to sit still.

"What do you have to be nervous about?" Lyle approached them holding a tray of coffee cups. Maybe he anticipated a long night.

"I'm nervous about the results."

Mom reached for her hand and gave it a squeeze. "No matter the outcome, we are family, and family sticks together. Right?"

"That's right." Carter took Nancy's other hand and laced his fingers with hers.

She glanced toward Gavin who sat in a booth talking with Maddie. Yes, no matter what happened they would have each other. Over the past few months she'd noticed a change in Mom. Maybe Lyle was the reason, or maybe it was her health scare. Whatever it was, she no longer feared what would happen if she lost the election. She knew Mom would be okay—even happy.

Mom gazed at Lyle. Love shone in her eyes. Would those two ever realize how much they loved one another, or would they continue to dance around their feelings? She hoped and prayed they'd come to their senses before it was too late.

Mom's and Carter's cell phones both rang. They looked at one another and reached for their phones. Nancy got off his lap. This was it. She held her breath as she watched their faces.

Carter gave nothing away as he pocketed his phone. Nancy's eyes sought his. What was going on? He wore a poker face better than anyone she knew.

Mom cleared her throat. "May I have everyone's attention please?"

The small crowd silenced and turned their attention toward Mom and Carter who now stood at her side.

"The election results are in. With eighty percent of the votes counted Carter has been declared the winner."

A murmur rose in the room.

"I personally want to be the first to congratulate my son-in-law. He will make a fine sheriff. It's been a long few months, and I'm glad to be on the other side of this election. Congratulations, Carter." She shook his hand. "The room is yours."

Lyle stepped forward. "Before he does, may I have the floor?"

"Of course," Mary said.

Lyle pulled a little box from his pocket and bent down on one knee.

Nancy gasped. Was this really happening? She looked around at their friends and noted their stunned expressions—yep. This was for real.

"Mary, I love you with all my heart. I want to spend the rest of my life with you doing whatever makes you happy. Will you marry me?"

"Absolutely." She held out her left hand.

Lyle stood and slipped the ring on her finger.

Everyone burst out in applause and whistles, including Nancy. Those little sneaks. Had they been seeing each other secretly? That would explain the change in her mother.

Carter clapped him on the back then shook his hand. "Way to steal the show."

"Sorry, buddy."

Carter chuckled. "No problem."

Mom and Lyle held hands and strolled to a quiet corner of the shop. Emotions she couldn't identify flooded Nancy. Her mom was engaged and her husband was slated to be the next sheriff. She rested a hand on her abdomen.

Cater addressed their friends. "Thanks to all of you for supporting us and coming out this evening. I hope to live up to the expectations of each and every one of you. I can't promise to be perfect, but I will do my best to serve and protect."

Everyone clapped, including Mom and Lyle. Nancy stepped to Carter's side and slid her arm around his waist. "Are you ready for how much our lives are about to change?"

"I'm not sure. When your mom asked me to run against her, I never dreamed I'd actually win."

"But now that you have…?" Nancy looked at him expectantly. He did want this, didn't he?

"Now I'm excited, and…"

"Terrified?" Nancy raised a brow.

"I wouldn't go that far, but uneasy. Your mom is leaving behind some big shoes to fill. I only hope I don't disappoint the people of Tipton County."

"Oh, I'm sure there will be a few naysayers. That's to be expected, but I have complete faith in you. I also have a little news of my own."

"What's that?"

She cupped a hand around her mouth and whispered into his ear. "I'm pregnant."

"What! I thought you weren't ready." Concern echoed in his voice.

"So did I, but I'm excited."

He frowned.

"What's wrong? I thought you wanted to be a dad."

"I do, but the timing is a challenge. I take over as sheriff in January and the baby will come…?" He looked to her for an answer.

"In July. You'll have six months to settle in before our little one makes an appearance."

A slow grin spread across his face. He cupped her face between his hands. "I love you."

Joy bubbled at his happiness. "I love you too." She kissed him soundly. "Should we tell everyone?"

"Not tonight. I want tonight to just be ours." He kissed her again.

Forgetting why she ever had a problem with public displays of affection she kissed him back with all the love that filled her heart for this man.

Author Note

Throughout the writing of this series, I knew that Sheriff Daley needed a book of her own. Through my years as a writer I've had many readers state they'd like to see an older character as the main character, but I never felt qualified to write one since I didn't know what it felt like to be older. Well...fast-forward to present day and guess what? I have a clue now. I turn 50 this year! Mary Daley and I are quite close in age, and it was time to give Mary her own point of view. I hope you enjoyed getting into her head.

I've loved writing this series—at least most of the time. I'll never forget the day the idea for *The Sleuth's Miscalculation* came to me. Writing those opening scenes were so much fun! This series idea sat on the proverbial back table for years before it was ever sold. You see, I had only written the opening scene for book one with an idea for the series. When my schedule finally opened up, I pitched The Librarian Sleuth series to my publisher, and she loved it. I hope you have enjoyed it as much as I have!

If that's the case please tell your friends and family about this series, and if you have a few minutes, I'd be grateful if you would leave a review.

Blessings to you and yours. Keep reading!
Kimberly Rose Johnson

Learn more about Kimberly and her books at kimberlyrjohnson.com

More Books by Kimberly Rose Johnson

Protection Inc.
Direct Threat
Imminent Threat

Law Enforcement Heroes
Edge of Truth

The Librarian Sleuth
The Sleuth's Miscalculation
The Sleuth's Dilemma
The Sleuth's Conundrum
The Sleuth's Surprise (September 2020)

Brides of Seattle
Until I Met You
The Reluctant Groom
Simply Smitten

Melodies of Love
A Love Song for Kayla
An Encore for Estelle
A Waltz for Amber

Sunriver Dreams
A Love to Treasure
A Christmas Homecoming
Designing Love

Wildflower B&B Romance Series
Island Refuge
Island Dreams
Island Christmas
Island Hope

Contemporary Inspirational Romance Collection
In Love and War

Contemporary Novellas
Brewed with Love
Sara's Gift